Praise for *The Bacon Fancier*

"The stories are slyly amusing, shrewd in social understanding and period detail, and rich in literary reference. They are a pleasure to read."
—Phoebe Adams, *The Atlantic Monthly*

"A subtle book, the writing endlessly nuanced . . . and yet, and here is Mr. Isler's strength, the stories are also funny, bawdy, and entertaining. One of the most exciting fiction writers to have emerged on the scene in the last few years."
—Jonathan Wilson, *The Forward*

"Isler has a remarkable gift for catching the small telling details of a character and for creating intelligent, distinctive voices. . . . By turns angry, deeply inventive, and unsettling, these novellas are a penetrating and original meditation on the vexed question of identity and a pointed reminder that Isler is swiftly becoming a writer of very considerable powers."
—*Kirkus Reviews*

"*The Bacon Fancier* attacks difficult and complex issues—exile, assimilation, anti-Semitism, ghettoization—with charm and flair and a manic comic edge."
—Gabriel Brownstein, *The New Leader*

"A dizzyingly erudite and dazzlingly funny new collection."
—Nicholas Nesson, *Boston Phoenix Literary Supplement*

"Wry, witty, and wise . . . a literary treat."
—Linda Simon, *Daily N*   *York)*

PENGUIN BOOKS

THE BACON FANCIER

Alan Isler was born in London in 1934 and came to America as a young man. He taught English literature in New York City for twenty-five years. His first novel, *The Prince of West End Avenue*, won the 1994 National Jewish Book Award and was one of the five fiction finalists for the National Book Critics Circle Award. His second novel, *Kraven Images*, was published in 1996. *The Bacon Fancier: Four Tales* appeared in 1997. He now lives in London.

PENGUIN BOOKS

Published by the Penguin Group

Penguin Putnam Inc., 375 Hudson Street,
New York, New York 10014, U.S.A.
Penguin Books Ltd, 27 Wrights Lane,
London W8 5TZ, England
Penguin Books Australia Ltd, Ringwood,
Victoria, Australia
Penguin Books Canada Ltd, 10 Alcorn Avenue,
Toronto, Ontario, Canada M4V 3B2
Penguin Books (N.Z.) Ltd, 182–190 Wairau Road,
Auckland 10, New Zealand

Penguin Books Ltd, Registered Offices:
Harmondsworth, Middlesex, England

First published in Great Britain as *Op. Non. Cit: Four Tales*
by Jonathan Cape Random House 1997
First published in the United States of America by Viking Penguin,
a division of Penguin Books USA Inc. 1997
Published in Penguin Books 1998

1 3 5 7 9 10 8 6 4 2

THE LIBRARY OF CONGRESS HAS CATALOGUED
THE VIKING EDITION AS FOLLOWS:
Isler, Alan.
The Bacon Fancier: four tales / Alan Isler.
p.   cm.
ISBN 0-670-87407-8 (hc.)
ISBN 0 14 02.6379 9 (pbk.)
Contents: The monster—The bacon fancier—The crossing—The affair.
I. Title.
PS3559.S5206   1997
813′.54—dc20   96–46227

Printed in the United States of America
Set in Perpetua
Designed by Jaye Zimet

FiCTION

JUN 2 3 1998 A

110549

The Bacon Fancier
Four Tales

Alan Isler

PENGUIN BOOKS

For,
in order of appearance,
Adam, Eric, Joshua and Claudia

Contents

The Monster

At one time a monster, a prodigy, was born in the Ghetto—well, not born here perhaps—we can't be sure—but discovered here certainly. The depositions before the Cattaveri are still extant. It happened like this. One afternoon, about two o'clock, the Cannaregio gate already closed, Simcà, the wife of Isacco Levi, a woman well advanced in middle age—dead now, of course—was returning to her home from an excursion to buy bread for her table. Passing under the portico of the Scala Matta, she almost stumbled in the dimness over a basket. *"Shema Yisroel,"* she said, "what now?" She was heard by Salomon Penso, also now dead, who was returning from the Calle Sporca, where he had gone to relieve himself, and who almost fell over Simcà, bent over the basket. Her voice stopped him short, but in any case, he could not prevent his codpiece from making light contact with her rump. "Excuse me," he said politely.

"Look at this," said Simcà.

"It's a basket," said Penso. "What's in it?"

"I'm afraid to look."

"We'll both look," said Penso. "But first let's carry it out into the light."

And thus Simcà and Penso became the first in our community, so far as is known, to look upon Mostrino, the Defender of the Jews. Together they pulled back the little blanket. Simcà shrieked. Later she would say that had she been a Christian, which thank God she was not, she would certainly have crossed herself. As it was, she had to content herself with "*Shema Yisroel,* it's a monster!"

What they saw was certainly ugly, an infant whose huge head was sunk in rounded shoulders, whose lower jaw thrust forward and sucked greedily on the upper lip, whose nose was the size and color of a small, ripe plum, whose scalp and forehead were matted with dark hair, and whose padded right fist waved aloft, thrusting at the sky the only three fingers it had.

Simcà's first instinct was to run, but Penso held her by the arm. "It's only a baby, after all. It must be hungry, see how it sucks on its lip." Together they carried the basket to Ricca Benincasa, the wife of Israel Coen Tedesco, who lived opposite the Levantine School and who was fat with milk. They asked her if she would keep the monster for the night and nurse it.

A closer examination now ensued, and two discoveries were made. First, it was a male monster, and second—a wonder!—it had no foreskin. By this, I do not mean that it was circumcised. No, I mean that Mostrino had dropped into this world without a penile sheath. Clearly, this was a matter for the rabbis, and Penso ran to fetch them.

The rabbis were impressed. The child had been found like a Moses, they reasoned; perhaps it was destined to lead the Jews back to the Promised Land. The absence of a foreskin might be the sign of a prenatal covenant, establishing for Mostrino an immediate and vastly superior Jewishness. They took note of the three little fingers waving before their noses. Here was the letter *shin*. Could it be that in this mute way the child was indicating its holy mission?

On the other hand, the baby was deformed, a monster. Besides, it lacked the look of intelligence; in truth, it looked stupid. Remember, these were learned men, wise not only in matters of the spirit but also in the ways of the world. They knew that the offspring of unwed mothers were numerous in the Ghetto; foundlings, though rare, were not unheard of. It was better to proceed with caution. Accordingly, they issued a notice of excommunication against any Jew who, knowing something of Mostrino's origins, failed to come before them to testify. Meanwhile, the child would be maintained at the expense of the community. Ricca complained that the ugly creature had already chewed her poor nipples bloody and drunk her dry. Very well. The rabbis placed Mostrino in the temporary custody of a Jewish wet nurse. And after he had milked and bloodied her, he was placed with another, and then with another. His thirst was prodigious and his gums were like bands of iron.

Meanwhile, the notice of excommunication had spread through all the little towns of Venetia and beyond. No one came forward. Who could imagine a Jew not responding to a threat of excommunication? What, then, if the monster were Christian? If it came to the ears of the authorities that the Jews were secretly harboring a Christian infant, the violence that this intelligence might unleash on the Ghetto was too terrible to contemplate. The rabbis determined to notify the Cattaveri of the foundling.

The Cattaveri instituted an immediate inquiry. In fact, one look at Mostrino convinced them that the child could not have been born of a Christian mother. It was clearly the Devil's offspring, or the Jews'. Nevertheless, they took the depositions of Simcà Levi, Salomon Penso and Ricca Benincasa, and they listened to the learned arguments of the rabbis. Then they closed the case. Their judgment reads in part: "The Most Illustrious and Excellent Cattaveri Niccolò Caruso and Alvise Gigli, having reviewed the evidence in the matter of the newborn male found in the Ghetto on the fifth of the current month and year, and having duly and maturely reflected thereupon, have in unanimity determined that the aforementioned newborn male shall remain in the Ghetto, in the custody of the appropriate persons."

Thus did Mostrino, the Defender of the Jews, come to live and flourish among us, growing rapidly, so that by his sixteenth year he had reached more than six and a half feet and weighed over three hundred pounds. The ground shook to his tread. Ten yards of cloth could not cover his nakedness. Only his head had not grown. It sat on his shoulders like a cracked egg on the lid of a wine cask. Hair sprang in ragged clumps upon his misshapen skull; his poor face with its purple plum of a nose had long since set in a fixed and meaningless scowl. And he could not talk. Fierce grunts issued from his twisted lips as he sought for words he did not possess. His greeting was three fingers thrust to the sky, the letter *shin*. Mostrino was the Ghetto idiot, utterly harmless, invariably good-natured. The children loved him. A cudgel was his one possession, his toy, never out of his hand, and with it he played his innocent games.

The judgment of the Cattaveri did not go entirely unnoticed in the Christian world, however. Baldassare Piero Maria Bembo, Canon of the Cattedrale di Ferrara, published a thundering polemic entitled *Discourse on the Birth of a Monstrosity to the Jews of Venice*. "Think well what this portends, O Jews. Is not this monstrosity given as a sign that ye follow along twisted and wicked ways? From such as this may we not suppose that ye plot diabolical evil against us? Are ye not by this clearly possessed of Satan and his demons? Pay heed, pay heed, think well on this monstrous sign. It falls not to us but to you, wretched people of the duplicitous and intransigent Synagogue. Jews, O Jews, I implore you in the bowels of the ever-living Christ: convert to the one true God. . . . Here I end, desiring the salvation of this accursed people and my own grace." Thus Baldassare Bembo. Well, what was it but another scurrilous and vain attempt to bring about our conversion? I mention it only because, to my undying shame, the then Canon of the Cattedrale di Ferrara had once been my brother.

Yes, I had an elder brother once. His name was Michael, ten years my senior. When he was born we lived in

Rome—my family did, I mean. Everybody who knew him said that Michael was a beautiful little boy, and no doubt he was. My mother drew her breath from his smile. My father said his glance would bring a blush to the cheek of an angel. When he was still in his cradle it was already clear to the congregation that he would become a great rabbi, perhaps even the greatest, another Maimonides. His very first words were *"Shema Yisroel."* My grandfather's chest, I'm told, was swollen with Michael's cleverness. Another point: he was born on Rosh Hashana; his circumcision was on Yom Kippur. As you can imagine, it was an event, that circumcision.

Well, one cursed day in Michael's seventh year he was out alone, walking, his mind perhaps engaged in some knotty problem of the Law. But it may be he was merely whistling, or kicking a stone. Remember, although he was clearly marked for greatness, he was also a child. In any case, his steps took him past the House of Catechumens. An old priest sitting in a window, a skirted poof with rouged cheeks and carmined lips, lured him in, who knows on what pretext? Michael was an innocent child, angelic. What did he know of adult wickedness? In his experience a grownup was first to be trusted, then to be obeyed. So in he went.

We know all this because a Jewish peddler, ostensibly (and illegally) crying his wares in the vicinity but actually hoping to catch a glimpse of his daughter, who languished within, saw Michael enticed, saw him enter. Who can measure my parents' anguish? My father had to be dragged from the very gates of the House of Catechumens. My mother began then her screaming descent into madness. My grandfather died of the shock. The congregation petitioned the Pope himself, that accursed, smiling Julius, may he shrivel forever and ever in agony, but there was nothing to be done. My parents never saw Michael again. The Church had received a new adherent. In due course my father packed his belongings and his mad wife into a cart and left Rome for Venice.

The Christians have never ceased in their efforts my whole life long. Oh, I know all about conversion. In due course, conversion even became my trade, so to speak: florins into ducats, for example; schillings into sequins. Yes, yes, I converted them all. But myself into a Christian? No, most emphatically not. Still, perhaps a word or two more about conversion is in order. We can return to Mostrino in a moment.

I was born in Venice on the very day that Pope Julius, may his transgressions never be extinguished, caused the Talmud to be burned in Rome, a memorable day. More than one thousand copies of the complete Talmud, and many other books besides, both new and old, went on the pyre, great tomes and tiny pamphlets, sheets of sacred music, first licked and then consumed by the hungry flames, blackened wisps of the holiest of words ascending on the upward draught to the unpitying vault of heaven. My infant cries were lost in the general moan.

And who put him up to it, this unfeeling and intolerant man, this Julius? Yes, you guessed it: the Jews. The great sin was born in the Roman congregation itself, the hideous worm was nurtured close to the innocent heart of the bud. Three convertites whispered lies about the Talmud into the ears of the Pope, who listened, smiling. Scorning the Covenant into which God had entered with our forefathers, they whispered their blasphemies. Julius smiled and nodded, nodded and smiled. Then he gave his orders to the silent henchmen about him. These went out quickly and nimbly and broke into Jewish homes, tearing books from the trembling hands of the righteous. A desecration of this magnitude, of course, was reserved for the Sabbath; such a desecration feeds their gluttonous sense of propriety.

Soon the Pope's minions were scurrying like cockroaches over the entire Romagna. Books without number were burned in Bologna and Ravenna. The Jews ached and cried out, but where was there a compassionate neighbor to hear them? Where is there ever? The cockroaches scurried and whispered and spread their slanders. In Ferrara and Mantua, too, the books were consumed, the holiest teachings were belched in soot to the winds. And Julius had strung his plumb even over Venice. My father watched his entire library succumb to the flames. The gentiles capered and clapped their hands, gawked at the spectacle, held up plump infants to gurgle at the pretty fire, sold oranges and sweetmeats, picked purses, made of our unspeakable torment a sunshine holiday.

Such was the day upon which I was ushered into this woeful world, a day not exactly propitious, all in all, something of a black day, and rendered so, as I have said, by three apostates, three convertites, whispering into the ears of smiling Julius. You see, I have not forgotten my new theme: conversion is what we're speaking of now.

Another was born in Venice that day, like me in the Ghetto Nuovo, another was born in the very hour in which my mother, not quite in her right mind, poor soul, was in pain and tears convulsively thrusting me forth from the womb. Yes, another was born, one Asher Bassan, in time to become that most reverent, grave and noble Signior Antonio Bassanio. No, I know all about convertites. The Ghetto was not big enough for Asher; he had ambitions. "There are millions of them out there," he told me once, shortly before he left. "They own the earth. Can you blame me for wanting a piece of it? For that I'll suffer a drop or two of holy water." Of course, I remonstrated with him, but I knew it was useless. Well, it was his affair, after all. I swallowed my repugnance and wished him well. We had been friends; we were to become deadly enemies.

Why did he not die in his mother's womb, so that she could have been his grave and her womb his eternal vault? Why, O Lord? Yes, my friend became an *apikoros,* a convertite. And because of him my child, my Jessica . . . but no more of that. Let him burn, O Lord, in perpetuity.

How I do go on! As if any of that mattered anymore! Notice how all the old curses still roll off the tongue?

Well, perhaps my brother, Michael, was not so splendid after all. My father's memory of him was colored by his loss. And my mother, of course, poor soul . . . The fact is, I met him some years ago, Michael, I mean, at the time of my landmark trial, and he didn't strike me as a potential Maimonides. Tall, stooped and thin, with a sour face and pursed lips, he was in holy orders, as I have said; a canon, no less, a poof himself, powdered and rouged. I should speak well of him. He had come to Venice to save me. He couldn't know I didn't need his help. The law itself was my advocate. But there he stood, shamelessly fondling the plump blushing catamite by his side who carried his parasol, the shoulders of his black cope disgustingly dusted with whitish scales from his thinning gray hair. He would not himself enter the Ghetto. No, he had sent a gondolier, a knave of common hire, to fetch me, summoned me forth to a meeting in the Rialto. There he implored me to embrace Christ, not merely to save my worthless body but to achieve the salvation of my soul. Needless to say, I turned my back on him. So much for Canon Baldassare Piero Maria Bembo. I remember that he had flat feet.

How badly they wanted me to convert! Years and years before, not long after my father had recited the blessing *"Baruch she peterani,"* joyful in his sorrow that God had freed him from his responsibility for me; not long after, that is, I had read my portion and lesson, Maphtir and Haphtarah, from the almemar of the Scuola Grande Tedesca and delivered (to the unfeigned wonderment of my father and the undisguised boredom of the congregation) my *Derashah,* a discourse on the spiritual benefits of the temperate life; in short, not long after my bar mitzvah, I happened to be on the Rialto. It was a late autumn afternoon, an hour or more before curfew.

As I recall, I felt myself to be cutting no end of an adult dash. The eyes of Venice were on my new doublet and hose. I swaggered, one hand held negligently on the hilt of the nonexistent sword at my hip, my head erect, a young gentleman, the embodiment of studied *sprezzatura*. What an ass, eh? That's what it means to be young. Oh, I was very fine, very fine indeed. I looked all around me beneath lowered lids, showing a proper disregard for the rude multitude. My red hat was no doubt set at a jaunty angle, just so. Wait, wait, no, we were still wearing yellow hats in those days, like the Levantines. Red hats came in later, a modish innovation. Probably some senator or other found himself one day with unsold bales of red cloth in his warehouse. Let the Jews wear red, he said. But a clever sempstress could make the yellow hat quite fashionable by the simple addition of a black trim. Diamante, Father's "friend," had fixed mine for me. As I think back on it, it must have looked like a giant bumblebee squatting on my head.

At any rate, on impulse and in an evil moment I stepped off the street and through the open doors of the Foolish Virgins Wine Shop. It was cool and dim within, and it smelled of rancid lamp oil and vinegar, of sweet wood shavings and forbidden food. There was the murmur of conversation and the muted sound of private laughter; and in the corner a dwarf lutanist, a *pazzo* in motley, strummed and hummed. My eyes having become accustomed to the gloom, I took a few bold steps into the room, waiting for the noise to subside, waiting—such was my prideful innocence—to be noticed and admired. Perhaps I struck a lordly pose, or a lascivious one: at age thirteen, I was conscious of the girl who carried the flagons from table to table, her impudent young bosom, twin orbs, thrust high by her bodice, conscious too of the worm metamorphosing into Leviathan beneath my codpiece. Oh, the fire that coursed in my veins in those days!

The talk and laughter went on; the lutanist hummed and strummed, strummed and hummed. No one had noticed me, after all. The girl had disappeared. Should I simply call out for a glass of wine? I was afraid my voice would crack and betray me. But then a figure separated itself from the shadows in the furthest recess of the room and stumbled across the floor towards me, a drunkard bearing a basin of some evil-smelling liquid in his hand. He stood before me, or rather (curved like a meat hook) above me, looking down on my upturned face. I knew real terror then. I should have turned and left. An evil spirit held me. The drunkard swayed and sweated, his eyes trying with comical ferocity to focus on my hat.

"Thou art a J-J-J-Jew, and therefore d-d-d-damned."

Now I had been noticed. Now there was silence in the room. But it was a silence pregnant with merriment, a silence breathlessly anxious to be broken.

"P-poor J-J-J-Jew," he said, and he sobbed for me. "Damned, damned, d-d-d-damned, thou art surely damned." With his free arm he wiped his forehead. He puffed and sucked at the air, puffed and sucked, still trying to focus his bloodshot eyes.

I see him as if he stood before me now. Were you to feel my palm, you would find it cold-damp, wet. I live the horror again. There he stands, swaying, puzzled. He wears a greasy brown jerkin. His thin lips are flecked with spittle.

"Without d-d-doubt, thou art damned."

I looked about me. To my right a pair of priests, regular clergy, Dominicans, sat at a table and nodded in amused agreement. They knew the Jew was damned.

Suddenly my tormentor took his arm from his forehead, where it had been usefully employed wiping up sweat, and swung it in an arc above my head, sending my yellow hat flying to the door. "I shall s-s-save thee." (May his teeth, eternally renewed, be perpetually pulled.) He took his basin and dashed its vile contents over my head. "Thus I b-b-baptize thee."

The wine shop exploded in laughter.

Thus the People of the Covenant are ever mocked and derided. How long, O Lord? Mount Zion is desolate and over it the jackals run wild. Why wilt Thou quite forget us? Why hast Thou forsaken us these many days?

I wiped my eyes. The girl squatted and, in the extremity of her merriment, lifted her skirts over her head and revealed her private parts. All around me was laughter.

The clerics, however, were not laughing. They looked at one another, nodded, rose from their table, and made towards me. "All right, laddie," said one, "it's the Fondamentina for you." "Indeed, yes," said the other grimly, "denial of Christ our Lord now makes of you a heretic, not a simple infidel." "Come," said the first, holding out his hand to arrest me, "the Casa dei Catacumeni awaits."

I turned and fled. Behind me was the bark of cruel laughter, and the priests' cries. "Halt!" "Stop him!" "Heretic!" I ran, my heart thudding. I ran. What else could I do?

Were the priests serious, or were they merely having their fun? You decide. Such things had happened before. Children have been snatched from their parents on flimsier excuses, my own brother among them. A Christian had thrown filthy water over me and uttered the magic words. In their mad view I might indeed be a Christian.

In fairness to Venice, the Serenissima has never badgered her Jews, at least not to the full satisfaction of Rome and the Church. Here, the conversionist sermons prescribed by Pope Gregory VIII—punish him, O Lord, for his wickedness—have never been in vogue. Here, generally speaking, it is felt that violent measures in matters of religion tend rather to exasperate than to edify. Pity our poor brethren in Rome, and even in Padua! In Venice, the enforced conversion of children is regarded as something of a crime, something not done. Although if it *were* done, what then? Can baptism be undone? Fortunately, the Dominicans gave up the chase. But for my father and me, and for the community, there were some anxious weeks. The conversion of adults, after all, was regarded even here in Venice a consummation devoutly to be wished, and under Jewish law, remember, I was already an adult. Only consider the smug peremptoriness with which I was treated by a Venetian court years later, at the end of my first great trial, the time that I brought suit against Asher Bassan, or rather, to be accurate, against Signior Antonio Bassanio, the convertite magnifico.

He had prospered in his years beyond the Ghetto walls, unhampered by the pinching laws that hem us in. His argosies were big-bellied on the flood, filled with rich silks and precious spices. In every foreign mart his scutcheon flew; he towered as a merchant prince above the petty traffickers. In brief, he'd cast his net around the globe and with it drawn in gold.

And yet one day he came to me for money. He would not tell me why he needed money or, needing it, why he came to me. That was no affair of mine. But he would sign a three-month note for three thousand ducats. Was I interested? Three thousand ducats! A tidy sum.

He had brought with him a friend, whom he introduced simply as Messer Orlando Lorenzacchio. This was a young fop, clad in blazing silks, an exquisite, whose hair was curiously curled, whose eye was disdainful, and who was perfumed like a harlot. In his hand he held an orange, and ever and anon he took it to his nose as if to protect that orifice from the vile air.

"Well, will you take the note?"

I said I would be honored.

The gilded waterfly whispered in Antonio's ear.

"As a usurer and a Jew," said Antonio, "you will no doubt expect to make a profit from this loan?"

"As a merchant and a Christian," I said, "you no doubt

expect to make a profit from your merchandise. Or do you give your goods away in Christian charity? But from you, Signior Antonio, I intend to take no interest. I'll lend you the ducats for old friendship's sake."

He did not like the word "friendship." "Most kind," he sniffed.

Lorenzacchio whispered once more in his ear.

"But we must put something down to make the note good," said Antonio. "Well then, I have it: for a merry jest let's say that, should I fail to meet my day, you are to cut from near my heart a pound of flesh. What d'you say?"

"A merry jest?" He disgusted me. "I cannot see the humor in it."

"Come, come, I insist."

"We must go to the notary." Would he had never stepped across my sill!

I called for my daughter, Jessica, to tell her I must go out. She curtsied prettily before the strangers. My wife had died giving life to her. Thus Jessica's beauty was for me a cause of joy and sorrow.

Antonio, I saw, was taken aback. He could remember Leah when she, like Jessica, had been sixteen. He bowed gallantly before her. "Your loveliness gives certain proof of your fair maternity."

Lorenzacchio whispered again in Antonio's ear. This time I heard his words: ". . . and proves that that old devil wears horns." They laughed together, the fop holding his orange before his nose.

I did not like the speculative way young Lorenzacchio's eye roved over my daughter. I did not like her simpering response, her blush, her smile. I hastened the gentiles out of my house.

At the notary's Lorenzacchio took the note from Antonio's hand, read it over carefully, smirked, and gave it back. Antonio signed. Lorenzacchio whispered in Antonio's ear.

"Would you care to dine with us tonight, you and your fair daughter?" said Antonio.

"The Signior is too kind. Alas, we may not, even if we would."

And that was that.

Time passed. Antonio's day came and went. At length I betook myself to his grand palazzo, bearing his note in hand. He fobbed me off, pleading for one week more. Again I went to him, again was fobbed. The third time I appeared at the palazzo, his servants thrust me roughly from the door, and from an upper window a cackling crone emptied a bucket of slops on my head, a second baptism. The urchins of Venice chased me home, hooting and screaming with laughter. So much for "old friendship."

I took him to court, justice my only plea. It was the first of my trials, a landmark case, for here was a reprobate Jew suing a Venetian, a Christian, a merchant prince—an unspeakable effrontery! The courtroom was packed. I stood for myself, Antonio's note my suit, his obligation patent. But Antonio was represented by old Bellario, the shrewdest lawyer in Venice, and seconded by young Lorenzacchio, no longer a peacock gallant but a lawyer's clerk in sober garb, a quill behind his ear.

I lost. It appeared there was an ancient law, buried in dusty books, that if a Jew should threaten the life of a Venetian, the Jew's own life was forfeit. The pound of flesh in the indenture was just such a threat. I pleaded in vain that I had no wish for a pound of flesh, that I wanted only my principal. So much for justice. The court then showed me mercy: I could render my life to the public hangman or I could enjoy my life as a Christian. I had a month in which to choose.

The rafters of the courtroom rang with the plaudits of the witnesses to my defeat. Bravo! Bravo! Antonio flung his arms around young Lorenzacchio and kissed him on both cheeks. Then he turned to me, a smile of cruel triumph on his lips and in his eyes the glint of guilty malice. I fled the courtroom with Christian shouts still echoing in my ears.

Of course, I appealed. My second trial proceeded without fanfare. The courtroom was almost empty. This time it was I who had engaged old Bellario. This time there was no smirking Lorenzacchio present; Antonio himself was represented by his chief steward. This time I won. Old Bellario, rummaging among his dusty books, had come upon laws that overrode the first. The threat of death or conversion was lifted from me, and Antonio, through his steward, was directed to repay me my principal—less court costs, which belonged to the state. I thanked the court for its justice, thanked old Bellario for his able arguments, and left.

My triumph was short-lived. I arrived home to find my daughter gone. Gobbi, my servant, told me that Messer Lorenzacchio had come to fetch her and she had shown him where I hid my treasure chests, which they had taken with them.

"And you made no effort to stop them, you imbecile?"

"They told me you had present need of your treasure, master, and you had directed them to carry it with haste to the court."

I feared my legs had turned to water. A terrible pain pierced my heart. Panting, I sent Gobbi for a little wine.

"You have seen this Messer Lorenzacchio before?"

"Yes, master. The first time when he came with Signior Antonio, and you yourself spoke very courteously to him. But many times thereafter, when he was sweetly entertained by my young mistress."

I made no attempt to pursue them. From time to time word reached me of their riotous living, their squandering of my treasure, in Genoa, in Milan, in Padua. I had a daughter, Jessica, once. . . .

But let us return to Mostrino. How we old men digress! And yet it may soon appear that I have not strayed so very far from my theme.

Once I was accosted in the Ghetto itself, right outside in the campo. It was noon on a sweltering midsummer's day. The campo burned like Gehenna. As always the high walls of the Ghetto kept any cooling ocean breeze from us. Indoors, of course, in shadow, behind shutters, it was bear-

able. A Jew could even breathe; with luck and God's blessing he might even possibly slumber. My own apartment,
high up, has windows opening onto the Outside, boarded
up in obedience to the law, or seemingly so. Naturally, I
always have them open at midday in summer, for who is
abroad then to report me? And what with the windows that
open onto the Ghetto-side, I enjoy sometimes a pleasant
crumb of a zephyr, not much, but nevertheless something.

In any case, on this particular day and at this inhospi-
table hour I was in the campo. Some business took me forth,
no doubt, but I no longer remember what it was, and it
scarcely matters now, since I was prevented from accom-
plishing it. That it must have been urgent the noonday sun
can attest. I made my way by hugging the walls and stealing
what little shade there was.

From the middle of the campo came the wretched yap-
ping of the mad dog Rabbi Shmuel of Frankfort had left
here two years before, an Ashkenazi dog shaped like a
stuffed sausage on four stubby legs—a *Pechel,* I believe they
call it. The dog wasn't mad when the rabbi brought it here;
nor yet was it mad during the memorable Pesach week he
spent with us. The dog went mad only when it was left
behind. Rabbi Shmuel had business in Ferrara and expected
to return for the dog within a fortnight. The rabbi never
returned. Subsequent inquiries revealed he had never arrived in Ferrara. Since the disappearance of Jews in transit
was not an unheard-of phenomenon, we could only shrug
and inly mourn.

Meanwhile the dog went mad. It fell into a sadness,

then into a fast, thence to a watch, thence into a weakness, thence to a lightness, and by this declension, into the madness wherein it now raved. The community fed it on scraps. Could we let the dog of the pious Rabbi Shmuel of Frankfort starve? It had become a charity case, another mouth to feed. We called it Frankfort after its place of origin. It had grown fat among us: its middle swayed from side to side kissing the ground as it trotted along.

At the moment Frankfort was snapping at the ankles of an Englishman who stood arms akimbo in the full glare of the sun, watching its frantic little leaps and terrified sinuosities with apparent amusement. Frankfort would not actually bite, you see. Eye rolling and incontinent yipping were the limits of its bellicosity. But the creature put on, one would have thought, a pretty good show. Nevertheless, the Englishman watched on, undisturbed. Poor mad Frankfort was forced to pause for a moment, panting, tongue hanging out and steaming, the middle of its fat tummy actually pumping the campo's stones.

I knew immediately from his attire he was an Englishman. He was appareled in colors brighter than the plumage of the Indies' bird, the parrot, and he imitated at once four or five sundry nations in his clothing, to wit: a Dutch bonnet, sky blue; French hose, bottle green; an Italian doublet, yolk yellow; and, despite the stupefying heat, a red-and-white striped Spanish cape. Nor did he seem to sweat.

I have always rather liked the English of all the gentiles and have spent many happy months in their wet and fertile country—secretly, to be sure, for as you must know, Jews are not permitted to live openly among them. Once I traveled there as a merchant from Muscovy, once as an Albanian goldsmith. But that is a story for another time. Suffice it to say, they are mad, the English, most of them, which truth may perhaps explain this Englishman's calm in the face of Frankfort's demented attacks. For Frankfort, having rested, was once again leaping about and yip-yapping.

"Quiet, mad Frankfort," I called.

Frankfort paid no attention. The Englishman, however, shaded his eyes with his hand and peered across the campo, where, in the small shade afforded by the second-story overhang of the abode of Benjamin ha-Levi, I stood sweating.

"Ho, sirrah Jew!" he called. "Hither, I say." And standing his ground, Frankfort yip-yapping at his heels, he beckoned grandly to me.

I shrugged after the Levantine manner and pointed a puzzled finger at my breast.

"Thou hast it, varlet. I would have word with thee."

What could a Jew do in those times (or in these)? Sighing, I walked out into the glare and over to him. "Yes, Your Worship?"

He was a young man of perhaps thirty, who wore his hair cut long and his beard uneven and unkempt. His nose was large, pockmarked and purple. Yes, I was right: he did not sweat.

Since he had summoned me in English, I responded in English, an ugly language lacking the mellifluousness of Italian (I say nothing of the sacred tongue) but one in which I confess to a modest proficiency. "What would Your Worship? How might I serve Your Worship?"

He held up a grimy hand. The teeth God had left him were rotting. "Enough, fellow. I know no Ebrew, I; no, nor Italian neither. Dost perchance speak English?"

What language did he suppose I was speaking, the ass! Was his purpose to insult me? But I nodded, and in nodding sealed Mostrino's fate.

"Good fellow. Art thou native to this place?"

Once more I nodded, and, for good measure, pointed across the campo to my house.

"Ah!" He seemed relieved. "No doubt thou wottest what it is I would, what-what?" He smiled and nodded his head once or twice encouragingly.

I shrugged to indicate puzzlement.

"A God's name," he said to himself and raised his eyes heavenwards, "I've found an idiot-Jew." He sighed; he tried again. "Sirrah Jew," he said smilingly, unaware or uncaring of the vile odor his rotting teeth gave off. I stepped backwards; he followed after, nudging me knowingly, smiling the while. He spoke slowly and with precise emphasis. "Thou knowest, dost thou not, where a bevy of good bona-robas is hereabouts to be found, what-what?"

"I would Your Worship took me with him. Bona-robas?"

"Aye, bona-robas, fellow, or beagles, trulls, trots, drabs, queans. D'you not catch my meaning, sweet Jew? Strumpets, stales, harlots, punks, tearsheets, cock benders, pistol grippers, pen wipers, cod swallowers, daughters of the game—in short, bona-robas, thou oafish Jew-fellow!" He smiled again, drawing breath. "Thou knowest, dost thou not, good Jew's son, where a bevy of them is to be found?"

"Your Honor is much mistaken. This is the Ghetto Nuovo, wherein live the Jews of Venice."

"What, what-what? Jew's-town, thou wouldst say?"

"Yes, Your Honor."

"No bona-robas here, eh what?"

"None, Your Honor."

"I see, ahem. Rascally boatman! Yes, quite. Ahem."

Frankfort meanwhile continued his crazy yip-yappings and insane leapings about. "Quiet, mad Frankfort," I said again. The Englishman, his arms folded now, one hand combing his tattered beard, a look of absentminded stupidity on his face (a common English expression), hauled back his foot and kicked the dog a powerful kick just beneath its tail. Frankfort ceased immediately his yip-yapping, a silent martyr. For the smallest part of a moment he stayed where he was, getting shorter and shorter and plumper and plumper. But then, quite suddenly, he took to the air, expanding to his full length, and sailed across the campo, heading for the blessed shade of Benjamin ha-Levi's overhang. He landed neatly on all fours, still silent, curled up, and went straight to sleep. The English, as is well known, have a way with dogs and other animals.

The Englishman now put his hand upon my shoulder, poking his thumb deep into the hollow above the clavicle and causing me thereby an exquisite pain. He looked at me very earnestly and said, "Tell me, Jew, what thinkest thou of Christ our Lord, and wherefore receivest thou him not for thy Messias?" He stood there shaking his head sadly. "Speak, Jew."

"Any gondolier, Your Worship, will be honored to take Your Worship to the bona-robas. Venice hath bona-robas enough for any taste, however discriminating. Your Honor needeth but tell the wretch what Your Worship desireth: dark or fair, old or young, cruel or kind, rich viands for a prince or thin scraps for a pauper. Do but let him know what you would, and your trusty Venetian gondolier will for the smallest of coins convey Your Worship thither. Come, Your Worship, I am myself even now going from the Ghetto. Let me lead Your Worship to an honest gondolier."

With a cunning squirm, as if I would turn towards and indicate the Porta to the south, I managed to release my shoulder from his cruel grasp. "This way, Your Honor." But he caught me now by the upper arm and squeezed my poor biceps very painfully.

"Come, let's hear thee, Jew. Come, what sayest thou of Christ?"

"But the bona-robas, honored sir?"

"To them anon; for now, our Savior." He squeezed, if it may be imagined, even harder.

"I think forsooth that Jesus was a great prophet and in that respect as highly to be esteemed as any prophet amongst the Jews that lived before him."

27

"So said the Turk at Lyons," mused the Englishman to himself in slow wonder. Mercifully he slackened his grip. But of a sudden he became earnest and peremptory. "We Christians do—and will even to the effusion of our vital blood—confess him to be the true and only Messias of the world, seeing he confirmed his doctrine while he was here on earth with such an innumerable multitude of divine miracles, which did most infallibly testify to his divinity." He caught his breath. "What sayest thou now?"

And there you have it, the curse that has been my lot through a long life. Once more I was marked for this misfortune. Out of doors in the pestilential heat of the noonday sun, innocent of harmful intent toward any, scurrying about my private affairs while others, more fortunate, slept—a polite and charitable effort to spare a stranger the frantic attentions of mad Frankfort, and what happens? I am caught in the fast gripe of a lunatic Englishman eager to embark on a full-scale Disputation. Here in the middle of the Ghetto Nuovo I come face to face with the Noonday Devil. His putative goal, of course, was my conversion. His actual purpose, I knew, was to furnish an interesting episode for his travel memoirs. I could see it as if I held the book in my hands: "I will now make relation of my discourse with the Jews about their religion. For whenas walking in the Court of the Ghetto, I casually met with a certain learned Jewish rabbin that spake good Latin, I insinuated myself after some few terms of compliment into conference with him and asked him his opinion of Christ, &c." There was no escaping it. The thing to do was to make him think he was getting his money's worth, an Interview with a Jew being the sine qua non of the Grand Tour that had pretensions to character.

"Perhaps, Your Worship, since we seem bound to dispute, you would permit me to lead you into the shade?"

He acquiesced but kept a firm grip on my arm. We walked some few paces.

"It cannot be," I said, "but that I address some magnifico of King James his court, a branch or sprig (as 'twere) of a ducal tree, perchance abroad upon an ambassade touching the Serenissima? Do I have you, milord?"

"Well, as to that, ahem, thou comest near me now." He smiled and swelled his chest as if he would split his fustian, besmottered doublet. Then he looked grave, stroked his beard, and frowned. We walked on. "No more of that, ahem. To *thee,* my sweet ounce of man's flesh, my incony Jew, to thee I am plain Tom Coryate, Englishman."

"*Sir* Thomas, I warrant, at the least, Your Worship."

"Peace, good pintpot. Peace, good Jew. A team of horse shall not pluck that from me."

"Well then, Sir Thomas."

"Ahem, Sir Jew."

"*Pocas palabras,* eh, Sir Thomas?"

"Peace, sweet Jew."

These civilities brought us to the shade hard by the home of Angelo Manoscrivi. Here it was possible to breathe.

"And now, Sir Thomas?"

"Eh, what? Ah, yes. Ahem." And he struck a pose as if he were addressing a vast multitude, his pockmarked nose a scant nine inches from my own. I see him now, one bottle-green leg thrust forward to assure him balance, one grimy fist clutching his Spanish cape, his other aloft, pointing a finger at the white-hot vault of heaven. "You Jews," he bellowed, "who are Christ's irreconcilable enemies, cannot produce any authority either out of Moyses, the Prophets, or any other authentic author to strengthen your opinion concerning the temporal kingdom of the Messias, seeing it was foretold to be spiritual. What say you to that, Jew fellow, what-what?"

I had time only to offer a pacific shrug before he went on.

"Christ does as a spiritual king reign over his subjects in conquering their spiritual enemies, which is to say the flesh, the world and the devil. Aha, I have caught you now upon the hip, Jew, have I not?"

A shutter flew open above us. "What's going on down there?"

"Only a disputation, Messer Manoscrivi. Nothing to worry about. An Englishman here wonders why I don't become a Christian."

"So it's you."

I admitted as much.

"What is it between you and the goyim? Didn't we have enough trouble with you the last time? It would be a blessing for the whole community if you *did* go over. Then perhaps an honest man could get some sleep."

30

"Who speaks there?" My Englishman joined me in the full blaze of the sun and squinted up.

"One Angelo Manoscrivi, a very learned rabbin."

Manoscrivi, in fact, far from being learned, was an ignorant clod. He was, moreover, the coarsest ruffian in the Ghetto, one who would as easily speak lewdly of the Holy of Holies as of his wife, or yours. On the other hand, he was a very charitable man, one who could be relied on to give generously whenever collections were made for the needy. Mostrino was a regular at his Friday-night table, and many other beggars besides.

"A learned rabbin, eh?" Coryate sneered, sneezed, and wiped the snot from his nose with a corner of his cape. "Bring the best of them before me. Let them break their lances on the compleat armor of Saint Paul. Ephesians, chapter 6." He raised a hortatory finger at old Manoscrivi and shouted, "The predictions and sacred oracles both of Moyses and all the holy prophets of God aim altogether at Christ as their only mark, in regard he is the full consummation of the law and the prophets." He paused only to take breath. "Look but at Esay, chapter seventeen, verse fourteen. Learn there of the name Emanuel and of a virgin's conceiving and bearing of a son."

"What does he say, the dung heap?" asked old Manoscrivi with irritation.

I translated.

"Tell him there is a privy place in his own anatomy wherein he may conveniently shove both Christ and the virgin."

"What says the rabbin?" asked Coryate eagerly.

"The rabbin respectfully suggests, Your Worship, that this and other passages of Holy Scripture are open to variable interpretation. It may be that you and he in honest thought do come to different understandings. So says the rabbin."

Coryate's eyes twinkled madly. He waved his fist about and leaped into the air as if he thought he might rise high enough to pluck Manoscrivi by the beard. "Abandon and renounce your Jewish religion," he screamed, "and undertake the Christian faith, without the which you will be eternally damned!"

Shutters were snapping open all around the campo. Jews were looking on, startled, sleepy-faced. A hum arose in the Ghetto.

"What's he want now?" Manoscrivi wanted to know.

Again I translated.

"Tell him," said Manoscrivi, chuckling, "that the same place in his anatomy where I bid him shove Christ and the virgin has room enough for him too, if he is only clever enough to sniff out the entryway."

"Well, well, Jew? Speak. Well, well?"

"The learned rabbin says only that he is resolved to live and die in his Jewish faith, hoping to be saved by the observations of Moyses his law. He has been too long embarked upon the flood, he says, to be willing to change vessels now, the port for which he makes being already in sight."

"Such is their insupportable pride," sighed Coryate, no

doubt addressing himself but content that I should hear him.

The noise in the campo had grown throughout this exchange. Coryate, deflated by Manoscrivi's evident and stubborn rejection of certain salvation, was becoming aware of
it. Jews shouted from window to window, some in fear,
some in anger, all in bewilderment. What was disturbing
their noonday rest? Everywhere infants were howling, and
even mad Frankfort had resumed his yip-yapping. A pot of
geraniums fell from a windowsill, narrowly missing Manoscrivi's head as it descended, and shattered on the stones
not a yard from where the Englishman stood. Coryate
started. He peeped about him through nervous lids. "Ahem,
what-what?" he said.

And now lumbering towards us across the campo came
poor Mostrino, swinging his cudgel in his hand, attracted
by the excitement, the noise, the stranger in his brightly
colored garb, all of which must have struck him as pos-
sessing the merry, chaotic quality of Purim festivities. He
wanted to be part of the fun. The ground, one would have
sworn, shook beneath his feet. As you can imagine, this was
a sight, first seen, to strike awe in any man.

"See, see!" cried my Englishman, gesturing at Mostrino. "What comes here, what m-m-manner of m-m-man
is this?" He gulped and stepped hastily back beneath
Manoscrivi's overhang, back, back, until he stood pressed
against the wall, spread-eagled, as if he meant to melt quite
through the very fabric of the house.

"Have a care, good Signior, sweet Sir Thomas," I replied. "Do not enrage him. This is the Defender of the

Ghetto, summoned forth by the cries of its Jews. He was created for us by our brethren of Prague, by that city's holiest rabbins. Four hundred pounds of Ghetto mud went into his making. The spirit of Samson by goetic charm brought howling from the black abysm of night invests his flesh. In his hand you see the Flail of Justice, carved from the jawbone of Leviathan. From his eyes dart forth the lightning's bolt. But fear not, for I am with you."

"I f-f-fear not, I, but that I stand here naked. Would that I had my t-t-true sword in my hand."

"Do not say so, my good Sir Thomas, do not say so! Rather give thanks unto your God you are not armed. For you must know that here within these walls our Defender is invulnerable, though powerless quite without. Here a battery of Switzers could not harm him. Speak you him fair, Sir Thomas, if you value your life. Speak you him fair."

For now poor Mostrino stood towering above us, his cudgel swinging gently in his hand. He scowled fiercely as always and emitted grunts. The spittle flew.

"Give you good day, good monster Jew," said Coryate, his eyes grown big.

"Rarrh-grroink-aargh!"

"Wh-what says he?"

"He would know why you disturb the Ghetto's peace."

"Tell I came but to admire the Ghetto and wonder at the beauty of its citizens, whose several virtues are known even in my distant land. I come not in anger but in love. All this I swear by Christ our Lord."

"Grrawh-arroingh-orrah!"

"What, Sir Thomas, mark how he rages! What, are you mad! Do not use the name of your Messias before him, lest he fall upon you hip and thigh!"

"By Moyses and all the holy prophets—by them I swear all that I have sworn! Tell him but that, and quickly, good Jew."

"Grr."

" 'Twere best, touching your safety, you took present congé from among us. The Defender when aroused maketh small distinction 'twixt Christian and Christian."

"I go, sweet Jew."

"Alas but that you must."

"But how?"

"I shall accompany you through the gate. I have some present business in Cannaregio. He will not follow us beyond the walls. But have a care. We dare not turn our faces from him. Yet thus, walking ever slowly backwards as from the presence of a prince or potentate, bowing ever low before him, yes, thus, thus, bowing once more, softly, softly, and yet another low bow, so, so, we may yet hope to see you safe beyond the Porta."

Thus did Coryate and I make our way, the poor monster stumbling after us, supposing perhaps we played some game, we retreating before him, the Christian in terror bowing ever low. The laughter from the campo rang sweetly in my ears.

Once we had passed through the gate, Mostrino set up such a howling and a brandishing of his cudgel, you might have thought him a whole tribe of murdering Caribs. Coryate turned and bolted for the Ponte Grande. I followed after at a more moderate pace. Mostrino, I felt sure, would not leave the Ghetto. One lesson had been seared in his small brain, this much at least he knew: his safety lay within the walls. Hence his horrible howling. He thought himself cruelly abandoned by his playfellows.

Meanwhile I joined Coryate before the bridge. "Fear not, Sir Thomas. As I have told you, the Defender is powerless beyond the walls. He stays where lies his strength."

Coryate set his Dutch bonnet to rights. " 'Twas not much to make an Englishman a-feared," he said. "Such bugs strike no terror in us. We fetch our line from Brut his men, who first rid our island of monsters." He flicked some dust from his cape with admirable nonchalance. "But true it is, the better part of valor is discretion. This fading mansion given us of the Lord, I mean the flesh, is not to be disdained before its lease be up. In natural piety, then, I removed my mansion hither, and I shall think the better of myself for it."

"You are point-device a man of valor, Sir Thomas."

"I thank thee, Sir Jew. Thus much being known, let us now repair us to the bona-robas." As you see, he was fully recovered. "I have about me a little bird that stirs, a phoenix in my conceit, that would find out a hidden nest of perfumed spicery."

A gondola was gliding towards the Ponte Grande from the east. In it I recognized Sir Henry Wotton, then the English Ambassador to Venice, his chaplain, the sanctimonious William Bedell, and a young boy, presumably Sir Henry's page. Since his royal master always kept a parsimonious hand on the privy purse, Sir Henry had had frequent occasion to avail himself of my coffers. In his behalf I must note he always cheerfully met his day. But now I had found an easy way to rid myself of Coryate.

"Hola, Sir Henry!" I called. "How doth Your Honor this many a day?"

"Hola! What news among the moneylenders?"

The gondolier slowed his craft. It slid beneath the Ponte and made for the bank. Coryate and I went toward it.

"Speak we of Sir Henry *Wotton*?" Coryate asked, slowing my pace. "King James his ambassador to the Venetians?"

"None other."

"Know you him then?"

"As you see." I produced once more the shrug of the Levantines. "Our acquaintance reacheth not, as 'twere, unto the first water, and yet it hath some luster to it."

"This is most fortunate. I have about my person here" —he patted his doublet—"certain letters of introduction to Sir Henry, one from my good friend Richard Martin."

"Come then, good Sir Thomas, let me make your presence known to him."

"Er, yes, yes, quite. . . . Er, it were best, sweet Jew, thou didst not . . . ahem. How might I put it to thee?" He plucked me by the sleeve. "My noble ancestor, ahem, Baron George Coryate," he went on, reddening, "took for his crest in old King William's time the motto . . . the motto, er, yes, *'Homblesse me lie,'* for which absolute gesture the Conquering William granted him and his heirs in perpetuity Odcombe in the county of Somerset. I am a twig of that great tree, whence comes it that for mine honor I dare not use my title before my countrymen. Make me known to Sir Henry as plain Tom Coryate. Let that suffice. He knows my worth."

With that we drew abreast of the gondola.

"What say you, my privy purse," said Sir Henry, lolling comfortably against his pillow, "will it please you to dine with me tonight?" He put up a hand to still Bedell's protest. The chaplain's thin lips were grim.

"Alas, sir, the articles of my foolish faith . . ."

Bedell's smile was sour.

"Well, drink some wine with me then. What say you to nine of the clock?"

"The curfew . . ."

"Fear not for that. Some of my particular household shall furnish you a safe conduct. I would have private word with you, some small matter that promiseth to benefit us both."

Another loan, of course. "I shall in all my best obey you, sir."

"Ahem, ahem, what-what," said Coryate at my elbow.

"Sir Henry, I had almost forgot," I said. "Here's one of your countrymen desires your better acquaintance. Lest you be in doubt, which, granted your sure knowledge and his rare parts, is not to be thought, here before you stands"—but even as I spoke, down went Coryate on one knee, off came his bonnet in an elaborate sweep—"or rather kneels one who humbly styles himself plain Tom Coryate."

One hand to his heart, Coryate flung the other toward the gondola, a thespian gesture which released his bonnet and sent it spinning like the Doge's ring into the water. He was undeterred. "Right honorable knight, ambassadorial star in His Majesty King James his firmament, my thrice noble lord, though I am confidently persuaded that I shall expose myself to severe censure at the least, if not the scandalous calumniations of divers carping critics, for presuming thus to address Your Lordship . . ."

"What means this commotion?" cried Sir Henry. But he did not mean Coryate's effusions. He was pointing in some alarm to the Porta. From there issued shouts of "Stop, Mostrino!" "Come back, come back!" And indeed, charging towards us was Mostrino himself, howling like an Irish kern, brandishing his cudgel in one hand, with the other pointing his three fingers to the sky.

Coryate leaped to his feet. " 'Tis the Defender of the Jews," he said, his voice quavering. "We are dead men."

I do not know what induced Mostrino to leave the safety of the Ghetto. But I suppose that seeing Coryate's bonnet hurled into the water, he thought himself invited to play, even as a dog will be seen to leap into a briar patch in pursuit of a stick carelessly thrown by its master. Instinct overwhelmed a lifetime's caution.

No sooner had Coryate said "We are dead men" than Sir Henry's page sprang from the gondola to the bank. What happened next occurred with such speed I was powerless to prevent it. The boy took a smooth stone the size of a plover's egg from a pouch at his waist. This he fitted into a sling, whirled the engine thrice above his head, and let fly the stone. Mostrino, howling and huge, was now no more than fifteen paces from us. The stone hit him with solid force in the middle of his forehead and stopped him in his tracks. For a moment there flickered in his eyes, I swear, a look of sharp intelligence and gentle understanding, but then the light went out, the lamp was spent. He staggered, his knees buckled, and he fell on his back, dead amid the settling dust.

"Well done, lad," said Coryate.

"Mostrino meant no harm," I said.

"Young Walter was very brave," said Sir Henry. "The monster surely threatened our lives."

"He was an idiot, a natural. He thought to play with us."

The boy had begun to blubber. No doubt, before today he had killed no more than sparrows with his sling. Now he had killed a man.

"It may be so," said Sir Henry, "but Walter acted in good faith to protect us. I see no fault in him."

And indeed, who could blame the boy? He had stood like a Philistine David against a seeming Goliath of the Israelites. As Sir Henry had said, he had been very brave. But now he leaped back into the gondola, resumed his place, and hid his blubbered face in his bonnet. He was, after all, but a boy.

"See, see, where come the Jews," cried Bedell, pointing.

Through the Porta came the Jews, slowly, in twos and threes.

"They come for the body," I told him. "We must bury our dead." I turned to Sir Henry. "Be so kind, sir, as to convey plain Tom Coryate hence."

Sir Henry nodded. Coryate climbed into the gondola. The gondolier, hastily crossing himself, made from the bank.

I walked the few paces to where Mostrino lay stretched out upon his back. From behind me, across the waters, I heard the excited voice of Coryate: "Four hundred pounds of Ghetto mud went into his making." I knelt beside the body, closed the dead eyes lightly filmed with dust. The jest had gone too far. The sweet taste of revenge had turned bitter in my mouth. Around the Defender of the Jews the mourners of the Ghetto gathered.

✾

But that was many years ago. Mostrino has been long turned into that dust from which he came, that dust to which, *baruch ha-Shem,* my own frail flesh will soon and at last be converted.

The Bacon Fancier

Who will look after me, now that Queenie's gone? Who will prepare my posset when the ague strikes and wipe the crudded rheum from the corner of my eye? And the puddings: who will make them for me now? Queenie had a way with puddings. The secret, she said, was in the herbs and spices. Blood pudding, marrow pudding, suet pudding, kidney pudding, batter pudding, bread and butter pudding, roly-poly pudding, plum pudding—Queenie made them all. The things she put in them! The things that I ate! My father, were he to know, would turn from me in his grave. The first time I saw her brushing animal blood over whatever it was she was stuffing into some poor dead creature's intestine, I blenched and ran for the privy. After that, I contrived not to watch her when she cooked. "Only don't tell me what's in it," I said to her. "If you want me to eat it, don't tell me." But they were good though, her puddings. "Why is it called plum pudding?" I asked her once. "It has no plums, only raisins." She looked at me as if I were a half-wit; she blushed in embarrassment for me, a foreigner with no sense. Who will make them now? And who will light the fire in the grate of a cold and blustery winter morning, warming the downstairs against my descent? Who will help me up-stairs to my bed, and chafe life into me there?

We buried her this morning, the Reverend Quintus Alcock and I—Poor Willie, the town idiot, alone in attendance—not in the churchyard, not in "hallowed" ground, but at the foot of the garden she had created behind the cottage. There we had years before buried our children, the born dead and the soon dead, unbaptized all. Never mind. As no less a worthy than Sir Francis Bacon reminds us, "God Almighty first planted a garden." But Queenie was the "Jooey Zoor" and hence did not merit Christian burial. Dr. Alcock, who liked Queenie—as, in fact, our neighbors had come over the years to like her—could not contravene local righteousness. She was, after all, the "Jooey Zoor," and liking had nothing to do with pious propriety. *That* was what they had called her at first, the women spitting the words at her, the boys accompanying the words with stones, the men nudging one another and winking, pointing her out in the street. I was at first not in command of the local dialect. It was a while before I un-derstood that "Jooey Zoor" meant "Jew's Whore."

I found her crouched on my doorstep one morning, a white face in tangled hair staring up at me with startled eyes out of a bundle of wet rags. The night before had witnessed a terrible storm, lashing rain, the wind driving in hurricane blasts, lightning flashes above the Bristol Channel. She had made her way through that, I later learned, fleeing from Exford across the moors and over Porlock Hill, alone and fearful, cold, hungry, and soaked to her very skin. What had driven her forth on such a night I would not be told until some years had passed. The morning, however, was calm enough, although the sky was grey and smeared with black clouds. I peered up and down the street; it was empty, save for a ginger cat that lapped at a puddle. "Come in and dry yourself," I said to her and put out a hand to help her up. She flinched from me as if she had expected a blow; I let my arm drop. "There's gruel enough," I said, "and bread besides. There's porter I can warm." She muttered something in that Somerset dialect that still seemed to me—out of London via (briefly) Bristol, and only one year in Porlock—a meaningless sequence of "zee"s and "arr"s and "orr"s.

Leaving the door ajar, I went back inside, returning after a moment with a bowl of gruel and a thick slice of bread that I placed beside her on the doorstep. She was like a small wild creature, wounded and timorous of human contact. I backed into the cottage and gently closed the door. Her startlement I had put down to my anomalous visage. Not expecting to find anyone on my doorstep, I had not as yet fixed my mechanical eye in its socket. She had never seen a Cyclopean man before, you see. The empty socket lacks something of God's plan for human beauty. But my mechanical eye, it is a wondrous thing, a delicate corn-flower blue, and thus quite different from the dark-brown lively one it normally sits beside. I got it secondhand, so to speak, at Barnstable Fair, fourpence ha'penny and it was mine. Alas, it is not a perfect fit, and sometimes falls out when I lean carelessly forward. The natural eye, which had fit very well indeed, I lost accidentally in a scuffle with one of His Majesty's press gangs in Bristol. When they saw what they had done and that I was no longer of use to them, they kindly left me in the doorway of The Jolly Tar, the establishment of a chandler who shared his premises with his father, a barber-surgeon. But I was talking of Queenie, was I not? By the time I had popped my mechanical eye into its place, heated a poker, and stuck it, fizzing, into two pots of porter, I could hear her scratching at the door.

She handed me the spoon and empty bowl— "Thank'ee, zur"—and turned to go, turned back, and pointed to the sign that creaked in the morning's breeze above my door. Her sounds implied a question.

"Ah," I said modestly, "that's me, at your service."

The moment lengthened. The puzzlement stood visible on her moon face. At last, I twigged. Poor soul, she could not read.

"It says, 'Ben: Cardozo, Maker of Fine Violins, &c.' There's more gruel yet inside, and the porter's hot." I turned from her and walked back inside. Like a stray lamb, she followed.

"You'll want to dry off before you go on your way," I said, shoveling some coals on the fire and poking it into more vigorous life.

She stood before me, a portrait of wretchedness, her

arms crossed and grasping her shawl about her, her skirts dripping a puddle onto the floor.

"Go into my workroom there and take off some of your wet clothes. Here's my greatcoat you can wear."

She shook her head, a look of fear in her eyes, and took a step back.

"There's no need to be frightened of me. I'm as harmless as innocence itself. Still, keep your wet things on if you want. At least sit before the fire." I handed her a pot of porter. "Drink this down."

I pushed a chair in front of the fire and backed away from it. After a moment's hesitation, she sat down, leaned towards the flames, rubbed her hands before them.

"That's better, isn't it?" I said. "You know *my* name. What's yours?"

She hesitated a moment, as if wondering whether she could trust me with it. "Queenie," she said.

"Excellent," I said. "A fine name for you. There you sit before the fire like a queen." (She smiled at this, the smile in the instant transforming her face. "There is no excellent beauty," says Sir Francis, "that hath not some strangeness in the proportion." Moon-faced she certainly was, ruddied by exposure to the country winds, but when she smiled she was a beauty.) "Queenie what?"

She frowned and shook her head.

"I shall call you Malke. That's 'Queenie' in the Hebrew."

She shook her head again, vigorously this time. Her name was Queenie, *tout court*. She was riddled with superstition was my Queenie, then and forever. For her, M. Voltaire might never have lived; the Royal Society, whose members had long been shining the light of modern reason upon medieval darkness, never have been founded. Malkin, it appeared, was the name of Mother Shipley's black cat, her familiar, and Mother Shipley, as everyone knew hereabouts, was a witch.

"Well, in that case Queenie it is."

She stayed, of course, although in that first chill dawn we neither of us knew she would. She sat before the fire all that morning, the steam rising from her in billows, misting the windows, turning the room into a species of Turkish baths, such as I had visited in Whitechapel, hard by the Commercial Road. In due course she fell asleep, her head fallen upon her small bosom, exhaustion from her flight across the moors and the damp heat at last getting the better of her. She slept like the child she was as Porlock began to stir, milk cannikins clanking, a cart axle squealing, the citizenry slouching past my door in unwilling greeting to the day; and like a child she dribbled in her sleep. I wiped the clear dribble from her chin and betook myself to my workshop, from time to time that morning peeping in at her as she slept. Towards noon I heard her stirring, heard the sounds of her activity, a besom whisked across the floor, the screeching of furniture moved, the creaking of cabinet doors, unidentifiable thuds and thumps, slappings and chitterings. Throughout all this I remained at my workbench painting, as I remember, a hunting scene on a lute ordered by a musical gentleman in Edinburgh, varnishing a viola da

gamba wanted by the *Kammermusiker* of Graf von Schmetterling of Kaumglück, repairing a violin first commissioned
by Giuseppe Maldonado, late First Violinist and Composer
Extraordinary to the Court of the Kingdom of Naples, now
an honored refugee in Vienna. By mid-afternoon a mouth-
watering aroma was teasing my nostrils. When the day
darkened into evening and I was about to light the lamps,
she knocked at the door, did not wait for my response, but
opened it, smiled, and triumphantly gestured behind her,
as one might to a foreigner who did not have the language.

She had so cleaned the room that it shone, it sparkled;
more, from the inchoate disaster of my larder she had prepared the first of her puddings, and much else besides. The
table was laid, the candles lit. I hunted out a flagon of wine
I had purchased from a Portuguese trader in Bristol the
previous spring, removed the seal, poured two tankards,
and we drank. We became merry, then merrier; another
flagon of wine was broached. The hour grew late. She could
scarcely resume her journey before morning—towards
Bath, as she had told me, and an elderly relative. The wine
had brought a fetching flush to her cheeks and slurred her
speech well past my limited comprehension. We both
lacked something of perfect balance in our lower limbs. I
offered her a makeshift pallet before the fire, which she
accepted, and I retired aloft.

In the middle of the night I was awoken by her screams.
In my nightshirt, I rose from my bed. She had been sleeping, not before the fire, but like a faithful hound before my
bedroom door. She had been beset by nightmares and cow-

ered now before me, grasping me about my knees as if
from them came her salvation. I raised her to her feet and
held her close, seeking to calm her terror. "It was no more
than a dream. There, there." She shivered violently, fight-
ing for breath, sobbing, sucking in air with animal gulps.
Still seeking to calm her terror, I drew her to my room.
My thoughts were honorable, believe me. She clung to me
as one in a shipwreck clings to whatever floats above the
swelling seas. At length, her shuddering sobs abated, but
she was cold, ice cold. I took her to my bed, yet wanting
no more than to comfort her, yet in honorable thoughts.
With my own body's warmth I stilled her trembling,
calmed the fever of her imaginings. She slept in my arms,
then woke and clutched me to her; slept once more, once
more awake. Before dawn had stained the window with its
light, she had become, with a joyful cry that must have
roused a neighbor or two, the Jooey Zoor.

She was then sixteen.

☙

I have not lived my life as a Jew, not really, not here in
Porlock. There is a mezuzah on my door, of course. But I
do not observe the holidays, not even the Days of Awe; all
these pass me by. Candles are alight on my table of a Friday
night, and of a Saturday I do no work. Still, I eat what I
eat, although before Queenie never pork, never shellfish,
never deliberately a mixing of milk and meat; and since
Queenie, well, as I have said, I found it prudent not to
inquire. Of course, as the year rolls round, I say kaddish

for my parents; that, at least, I have always done. And I have welcomed the infrequent visits of the occasional Bristol and, even less frequently, London Jew. My co-religionists pressed their fingers to my mezuzah and conveyed them to their lips. In my home they took only ale or cider or porter, bread, and salted herring. They talked of the small Jewish communities in this sceptered isle, in London, in Leeds, in Bristol, of the importance of marriage, Jew and Jewess, and of the few others, like me in isolation, the very few, scattered in the south and west, but married, so far as they knew, every one. What could have possessed me, they wondered, a young man, who, apart from a slight physical debility, enough perhaps to have denied me a priesthood in the ancient Temple—here, they smiled ironically—to separate himself from his fellows, to deny himself a helpmeet, the very heart and hearth of his home? (Queenie, who cheerfully plied them with that sustenance they would, at least, hungry, accept, who soon learned that her puddings and her most accomplished dainties were forbidden, not to say hateful, to them, they ignored as a nonpresence.) Why, in short, had I chosen to live alone in Porlock?

Why indeed?

I was born in the Ghetto Nuovo in Venice, the son of Leonardo Cardozo, master cabinetmaker, upholder of the faith, and of his wife, Fiorella, herself a daughter of rabbis. As the only child of theirs to survive childbirth, I was undoubtedly spoiled. All the potential virtues of their lost children they supposed to be gathered in me. They doted on little Beniamino, as I was then called.

In due course, I began studies for my bar mitzvah. It was discovered that not only had I been born with perfect pitch but I also sang with a voice of supernal purity and loveliness, a fitting solo for a celestial choir. My father, mindful of certain shocking stories then current, now feared that the Church, learning of my gift, would snatch me from him, baptize me, and then castrate me. He determined, in despite of my mother's pleas and his own sorrow, his natural desire to keep me with him and train me in his own workshop, to send me far away from Venice, to find for me some vocation that might combine my own gift with the one he believed I had inherited from him. Accordingly, my bar mitzvah now passed, he bound me apprentice to Niccolò Cipriani, master violin maker of Cetona in Tuscany, and tearfully, in a wagon laden with an ornate *scrittoio* bound for Count Malocchio in Chiusi, sent me on my way. Before I left, before, that is, my father tore me from my mother's arms, he made me swear not to sing again before my voice broke.

I never saw my parents again. One dreadful night, the Serenissima was battered by gales and pelting rains, small vessels were tossed onto the decks of mighty ships that themselves foundered at anchor, a mighty flotsam of masts and tackle seethed in the roiling waters and smashed in combat. Lightning flashed on scenes of violent desolation. In the canals the waters rose, exhaling a stench from the ancient silt, now in uproar, that the pounding rain could not beat down; anyone so foolish in such a storm as to traverse, for example, the Rialto Bridge would fight his way

through water swirling furiously at mid-thigh. The very pa-
lazzi yielded their lower floors to the flood. The bells in
the churches tolled maniacally, seeking in vain to quell the
deafening clamor of the storm. And on that night my father
was awoken from his sleep by a noise he supposed to em-
anate from his workshop immediately below his dwelling.
(This, and what follows, is what is supposed to have occurred.) Descending, trembling candle in hand, to confront
imagined villains, he tripped and sent his candle skittering
amid the pots of varnish, the glue, the stains, the sawdust
and the wood. The fierce conflagration that ensued took my
parents from me; the storm confined the damage to workshop and dwelling, a building that disappeared, leaving
neighbors on either side miraculously unscathed. That is
how it was.

Messer Cipriani was a decent fellow, after all. He had
three apprentices, Giuseppe, Lippo, and me, and a jour-
neyman, Enrico Perfavore, known as "il Gallo" because of
his dawn raids upon the virgins and former virgins of Cetona
and environs. My master was a superb practitioner of his
craft. An unbroken line of genius may be traced from Amati
to Stradivari to Cipriani. To this day a Cipriani, if one is
lucky enough to find one, is a wonder of the world. He
taught me whatever he knew of his craft. But Niccolò Cipriani was also a fancier of young boys. Not that his pre-
dilection interfered with his instruction, and besides, when
I worked under him he was already too old and infirm to
act upon his desires. But, at least before our voices broke,
he would require his three apprentices to stand naked before

him every Saturday night before bed to submit to an inspection of our cleanliness, our readiness to receive the
body and the blood of Christ on the following day. He
examined our fingernails, our elbows, our scalps, our teeth,
and behind our ears, but he paid particular attention to our
hinder cheeks and to our genitals. "What have we here?"
he might say, bringing his nose close to Lippo's rump. "Is
this how we prepare to greet the Son of God? Shame, O
shame!" And he would lovingly wipe the offending orifice
with a cloth dipped in attar of roses. Next came the turn
of our "darling little watering cans," as he called them, my
own, lacking a foreskin and hence requiring rather less attention, something of a disappointment for him. "Tsk,
tsk," he would say sadly, letting it drop, taking away his
fingers with just the slightest tickle to my scrotum. Giuseppe's watering can invariably grew erect during the examination, a happening that pleased old Cipriani: "What
have we here, eh? Tsk, tsk." And with his free hand he
would pat Giuseppe absentmindedly on the head. On Sunday mornings I was allowed to sleep late, spared, perhaps
by my father's initial arrangements with Cipriani, from the
body and the blood of Christ.

By the time old Cipriani lay on his deathbed, I alone
remained in his workshop, his other disciples having left
severally to make their own way in the world. Their way
must have been strewn with impedimenta; I cannot say I
heard of any of them ever again. Dying, Cipriani bequeathed
to me the secret of his varnish. He lay in his bed, his

breathing labored, his wrinkled visage stiff and waxen, his yellowed pallor flickering in the ghastly light cast by a single candle. "You are a good boy, Beniamino." He clutched at my hand and drew it to his chest. His eyes, red-rimmed, stared at nothing. He was already little more than bones assembled in a nightshirt. "Kiss me, Beniamino." Reluctantly, for he smelled bad, I bent over him and kissed his forehead. His skin had the consistency of yeast. "Go, fetch parchment and ink. The varnish. Write down the formula."

The truth is that in his last two years the violins and violas that left the workshop affixed with the label "N. Cipriani, Cremona," and the year, had been my work in their entirety. Except for the varnish. Until the end, the old man had prepared that himself, while I slept. Of course, I had known he had used a gum soluble in oil, quick-drying, or relatively so, and vegetable dyes; but the proportions—they were everything, and of them I knew nothing. The *tone* of a violin depends upon the varnish. That is what distinguishes an Amati from a Stradivari, a Stradivari from a Guarneri—and from a Cipriani. The wood is far less important. Of course, merely by the application of varnish, you cannot turn an ill-constructed violin made of inferior woods into a Cipriani. But a superbly constructed violin, made of the finest woods, will not have the tone of a Cipriani (or a Cardozo!) without the application of the superior varnish.

"No need for parchment. I shall remember your words

forever." I was much moved. Tears ran down my cheeks.
Here was a master, after all, who had become my mother
and father.

"Do as I say." His breath rattled in his chest. "Fetch
the parchment, the pen and ink. Write down the formula.
Then, fetch the priest."

I was bereft, an adult but once more an orphan. What
was I in Cetona without my master's protection but a Jew?
A cousin of my mother's, with whom over the years I had
kept in sporadic contact, had urged me often to join him
in London. In England, he said, a Jew could breathe free.
There were a few restrictions. I could not complete a university degree, to be sure, or become a Member of Parliament, but apart from that, I could ply my trade unfettered.
England was a musical nation, a host to Handel and the
infant Mozart. Come!

My Jewish attachments were already somewhat tenu-
ous. Not that I wished to embrace the Christian nonsense.
"Prosperity is the blessing of the Old Testament," says Sir
Francis; "adversity is the blessing of the New." Philosoph-
ically, I was something of a Deist, and, but for his raw and
painful hatred of the Jew, I saw much to admire in the
writings of Voltaire. But I was already a devotee of the
pellucid essays of Sir Francis Bacon, which at that time I
had read only in the translation of Gaetano Fellini. With
Sir Francis I had felt from the first a natural affinity. The
essays offered a guide to life and a comment on it. To live
in a land that had once produced such genius was tempting

indeed. Besides, I was young, and, as Sir Francis says, "Travel, in the younger sort, is part of education."

Within six months of my master's burial, all outstanding orders to the House of Cipriani having been completed to the purchasers' satisfaction, I closed the workshop in Cetona and made my way to London, specifically to the East End of that city, where, with my cousin's help, I set up in trade. London has many marvels and beauties, but not many are to be found in the East End—except, perhaps, for the Bevis Marks synagogue, which if not a marvel is nevertheless a beauty. But I, as I have said, a Deist, did not often frequent it. My co-religionists—if so irreligious a one as I may so term them—turned this way and that to find a suitable bride for me. It offended their sense of decorum that I, an eligible bachelor, should be in want of a wife. Many were the Friday-night meals I attended at which the blushing nubile beauties of Jewry curtsied before me, offering many temptations. And I was not—I state it as modestly as I may—an untoward prospect for any girl who favored parts over riches. But I wanted first to establish myself in a new land, create a strong financial foundation for marriage. "He that hath wife and children," says Sir Francis, "hath given hostages to fortune." Meanwhile, I assuaged my bestial longings on the lighter ladies of the town.

In due course, I was established; in due course, I made my way to Bristol. The occasion was the delivery of a violin to a young naval officer billeted there, one who admitted cheerfully upon delivery that he possessed only fifty percent of the agreed price, an unlucky evening at cards having deprived him of the balance, but one who assured me that not only would he be able to cancel his debt—prize money due him was already on its way—but he could (and would) deliver unto me other naval personages in need of my services. "There's not a moment to lose," he told me, with one hand taking the violin and with the other urging upon me a small bag of guineas and his list of names. "I sail with the tide." As it turned out, he had not deceived me, and I was, in the fullness of time, to receive from his factor the balance he owed. But it was this visit to Bristol that cost me my eye.

After the kindly ministrations of the surgeon at The Jolly Tar, I felt unable to return to London and the East End. Indeed, I was in a terrible way. Perhaps I was mad. Certainly, I felt a most extraordinary guilt, as if I were somehow to blame for my misfortune. Beyond that, I felt a kind of callow embarrassment: what would they say at Bevis Marks of my folly? Moreover, I was maimed, cruelly disfigured, and had no wish to parade myself before any who knew me. For months I wandered the highways and byways, the hedgerows, the coves, the hills and valleys, of Cornwall and Devon and Somerset, a harmless wild man, eventually a familiar figure to those whose charitable instincts gave succor and sympathy to wretches they perceived as less fortunate than themselves.

More than once I fetched up at Porlock in Somerset, liked the place, the people, and determined that there I would make my stand. The madness had left me. I was now

accepting of my condition. Porlock was but an English version of Cetona. I would move my workshop here. And so
I did, writing to my friends in London and begging them
to send my tools and other necessaries hither. I began again,
and began again to flourish. "Whoever hath anything fixed
in his person that doth induce contempt," says Sir Francis,
"hath also a perpetual spur in himself to rescue and deliver
himself from scorn." A Cardozo became a prized possession, not only in the United Kingdom but in all the lands
from the Peninsula to the Carpathians. My instruments are
to be found in the courts of princes, tuned in the hands of
master musicians, played with confidence and pride.

And then Queenie came to Porlock and to me. A lonely
and merely tolerable life became a life of warm content-
ment, companionable, and, in our early years, even passionate. "Nuptial love maketh mankind," says Sir Francis,
but he adds slyly, "friendly love perfecteth it." Friendly
love is what we enjoyed. But what a life had been hers!
Her mother, with Queenie already stuffed and thriving in
her belly, was married by a hedge priest to the supposed
father, a jolly rogue of a wrecker out of Lynmouth, who,
when Queenie was little more than five, died of a customs
agent's bullet in his throat. Queenie had few memories of
what in her mind were her halcyon years. She remembered
that her "father" had once made a coronet of daisies for
her hair. Thus, she thought of him, in her exquisite illogic,
as a species of poet. Her mother was married again, and
again by a hedge priest, this time to a swineherd of Exmoor,
a lout, a brute, but no more loutish and brutish, one sus-

pects, than is commonly the case among the lowest order of country humanity. Who can blame him, deprived as he was by ignominious birth of every precept of civilization? Nature, since the Fall, without the ameliorating influence of education, is much depraved, and man's life, as we are told by the best authorities, is cursed with misery. By such a yardstick, Queenie's stepfather was unexceptionable.

The experience of actually living with such a man was another matter, as Queenie and her mother came to rue. When he was sober, he was merely rough in manner, clumsy in act, and stupid in utterance; those were the good days. When he was drunk, he was a monster, beating his wife half-senseless before having his way with her. The hovel had only one room, and Queenie, trembling in her straw pallet in one corner of it, squeezed tight her eyes and cupped her child's hands over her ears. Queenie's mother, poor soul, was to die of a cancer that blackened and ate away half of her face. When, in her last anguished months, she was of no use to him, he brought, in his drunkenness, a sow into their squalid hovel and terrified her into holding the beast steady while he satisfied his black lusts. The sow he called Sally, after his wife.

"She was scarcely buried," said Queenie, "when he came after me." In sobriety, he would stumble through a grotesque parody of courtship, praising her titties, speculating on the juiciness of her maidenly treasure, and assuring her that the massiveness of his member would grant her pleasures she scarce could imagine; in his cups, returned reeling from the weekly fair, he would pound like a maniac on the hovel door, barred against his entry, the child within trembling in her dark corner, until, thwarted, he fell to the ground in deep, snoring slumber or staggered off toward the sty. One night, the night of the storm, he succeeded in breaking the hovel door down, but as it fell, he fell upon it and descended into an inebriate sleep of stentorian snores. That was the moment she chose to escape, her one defense, the barred door, now useless, and skipping over his sense-less form she gave herself to what she perceived the lesser evil, the fearful tempest, and made her terrified way over the moor and Porlock Hill to me.

As I have said, it was some years before she told me her story. For months she had feared that her stepfather would come for her, that our neighbors would in meanness pass a word along, but in time these fears abated; in time, too, her nightmares left her. From the first, she *took* to me, and I from the first was glad of it. She lacked all refinement, all pretension. She was herself. And if sometimes a mel-ancholy fit descended, she shook it from her, at least in my presence, as she shook her rich hair before the fire after a washing. And yet to have suffered so! She was—how shall I put it?—*discreet*. Great suffering requires discretion. She would not oppress me or caress me or distress me with it; she even feared she might bore me with it. And she knew that, however sympathetic, *I* could not feel her pain. It was her own, and she preferred to keep it to herself. And yet, Sir Francis tells us, "a principal fruit of friendship is the ease and discharge of the fullness and swellings of the heart."

One day, Queenie and I having already lived contentedly together for more than three years, I received through the good offices of my mother's cousin in London an order for a dulcimer. The instrument was wanted by a Mr. Solomon Mendoza, a wealthy merchant of Bristol, as a present for his sixteen-year-old daughter, Shoshana, or Susan, as they had Englished it. This Susan, according to the cousin, possessed rare beauty and every accompanying maidenly grace. Handsome young bachelors beat at the Mendozas' doors. Mr. Mendoza had been apprised of my honesty, eligibility and good parts and had declared himself not averse to considering my suit. We would meet upon the delivery of the instrument. Here was a match in prospect, wrote my mother's cousin, not lightly to be daffed aside.

I daffed it lightly aside—at least, at first. If I had regained any confidence in my attractiveness to the gentler sex, that confidence was attributable to Queenie, who seemed not to notice my deformity. No, I doted in mine own comforts. My interest was the dulcimer. I had made one years before under the tutelage of Messer Cipriani, and so I knew something of what I was about. But Mr. Mendoza wanted a *presentation* piece, not merely a *musical* instrument. According to his instructions, it was to include, inlaid in gold and silver and ivory, not only his daughter's name and age in English and Hebrew, but some design that pointed to her virgin beauty. These were the challenges that exercised my imagination. Cost, I had been given to understand, was not in question. What mattered was my artistry.

And so I labored. And in the weeks of labor I began to think. Having learned once more how to live, I wanted that life to continue. Moreover, I wanted it to live on in a son. Whence came such a desire? Perhaps it was inborn. I sectioned the wood, measured its thickness with calipers; I shaved it, bent it, set it. Not merely did I want a son, I wanted to raise a son in the ancient faith in which my own father had raised me. Whence came *that* desire? Perhaps it too was inborn. On paper I sketched designs for the inlay, scrapped them, began again. But what of Queenie? The mind is an instrument of wondrous flexibility. I turned the argument upside down. The point now was Queenie's future. By what right did I keep her here, reviled by her co-religionists, at my beck and call, devoted to my comforts, a pretty, a marriageable young woman yet, while the years sped by? I fitted the pieces of the dulcimer together, took them apart again, shaped the inlay, placed it. Were it not the kinder part—the infinitely kinder part—to have her join her aunt in Bath, provide her with the means of travel thither, a dowry, the expectation of a suitable marriage in a church, children the world would not condemn as bastards? I mixed the varnish, modifying the recipe, heated it, cooled it, tested it on scrap, rejected it, began again. Ah, but how could I deny myself the undoubted contentedness she had brought me? Deny myself I would, for Queenie's sake. (Says Sir Francis: "A mixture of a lie doth ever add pleasure.")

While the varnish dried on the dulcimer, a drying that in this damp clime calls on the last reserves of patience, I planned my journey of courtship. News had reached me of the *Bounty of Brasil*, bound for Bristol and wrecked in a storm off Lynmouth, a three-master that in its cargo bore certain rare Amazonian woods I had ordered from my Bristol factors. My woods, miraculously, were safe, but I would have to receive shipment in Lynmouth and make private arrangement there for their conveyance to Porlock. Accordingly, I proposed to walk the few miles along the coast to Ash Farm in Culbone Combe, where, as often in the past, I would take refreshment, and from there by farmer's cart to Lynmouth. In Lynmouth I would complete my business and spend the night at the Penrose Arms, famous for its potted char and game pies. The following morning I would prevail on old Ralegh, honest fisherman and dishonest wrecker, to sail me eastward along the coast to Bristol. In Bristol, the dulcimer delivered, I would take my measure of the Mendoza beauty.

At dinner I raised the matter with Queenie, waiting until we had consumed prodigious quantities of fish, roast duckling and Portuguese wine and a comfortable somnolence had descended. What remained of the meal was a rice pudding with plump raisins, a particular favorite of mine. It had been my intention to arrive at the nub circumspectly, speaking of my need for a true wife and hers for a true husband as if far off, a matter for leisurely discussion. In the event, I blurted it out.

"Queenie, I must have a wife."

At first, she misunderstood me. "But Ben, you know we cannot marry. There's no priest nor rabbi would splice us. Besides, what difference would their holy words make? We're happy as happy could be without them. What's their blessing worth, Christian or Jewish?" But then, perhaps catching the lie of my face, she caught a glimmering of my meaning. "There's someone else has taken your fancy, some vixen, some sow! You want to throw me into the street!" And she howled.

What could I do but comfort her? "That's not it, not it at all!" And I told her of my concern for her future, of *her* need for a proper husband, a settled life.

She laughed bitterly. "For my sake, is it? I'm to be thrown into the street for my own good?"

"You're not to be thrown anywhere. You shall have a dowry, become a fine catch for some handsome young man."

"Money! You've had me and now I'm to be paid! You're like them out there, no better. For you too I am only the Jew's Whore!"

Then the tears came, and wild choking sobs. I sought to comfort her, but she flung my arm away. I stood by helplessly, and then tried once more. She suffered me to touch her, to draw her to me. I held her close, kissed the top of her head. At length, the heavings of her body subsided. She was trying to say something. Gently, the better to hear her, I moved her head from my chest in which it was buried. She clutched me tightly.

"Why can we not stay as we are? I love you, Ben. I love you. I thought I had made you happy."

"And so you have, Queenie."

"Well then?" she wheedled, and pitiably, with trembling hand she reached for my manhood, willing, if that would keep me, to become my whore indeed.

I took that trembling hand in mine. "There, there" was all I could think of to say. " 'Twill be all right. No need of that."

Her face, made ugly by the blubbering, turned bright red. She howled and doubled over, clutching her stomach.

"What is it? What's wrong?"

"The cramp!" she screamed. "I must lie down! O God! O sweet Jesus!" She staggered to the stairs and pulled herself up them, leaving me standing there, not knowing whether to follow or to stay.

I stayed.

When darkness came I lighted my way upstairs. She lay, curled upon herself and whimpering, her back to me, upon a pallet she had fashioned and placed before our bedroom door.

"This is foolishness," I said.

She whimpered.

"Shall I heat you some broth? You should take nourishment."

She whimpered.

"Is the pain gone?"

She whimpered.

I shrugged, stepped over her, and took myself to bed.

Where was that grain of human sympathy that should have prompted me to lift her in my arms from where she lay, to have placed her in warmth and comfort beside me in the bed, to have spoken words, whatever words, that might have eased her misery? I was myself in mental anguish, fearful of breaking my resolve, of giving in to female tears, of saying "There, there, forget all I said, we shall go on as before." It was as if I stood on the edge of an abyss: to step back was to preserve my new-minted dreams of Hebraic domestic felicity; to step forward was to dash them forever on the alien rocks below. The paradox of my condition was this: I felt humble before her love of me, a love I could not doubt, and *that* drew me to her; I felt a diabolical pride in my power over her, the knowledge that I held her happiness in my hands, and *that* drew me from her. The result was a kind of stasis that kept me silent in my bed. Soon enough, the regularity of her whimpering lulled me to sleep.

In the morning, I descended to find her bustling about. She had prepared my breakfast in the usual way and a satchel of needments for my journey. Her face looked swollen but otherwise serene. Guilt stabbed at me.

"Look, Queenie, about last night—"

"How long will you be gone?" This was said cheerfully.

"A few days. But I—"

"I've been thinking, Ben," she said, handing me my mechanical eye, newly washed and shining. "Why should I not stay on as your servant? To help, you know, with the housework? Your bride will find me useful. She may even come to love me. And I, of course, will come to love my mistress." This was said calmly, albeit her eyes shone with tears.

"Oh, Queenie."

"Why not, Ben?"

"Two young women in a small house, the servant known to be no servant? Come, come, Queenie, what would the town think of that?"

For a moment her eyes flashed. "What does the town think at present?" But then she softened: "I cannot take your money, you know that. But I can take a servant's wages, and gladly. For otherwise it's the streets for me."

"But what about your own chances for happiness? Why should you not have a husband of your own?"

"I want no husband. It seems I'm not the marrying kind."

"Well, well."

"You'll think of it?" she said earnestly, her brow puckered.

What could I say? "I'll think of it."

I picked up the dulcimer in its finely crafted case. She handed me the satchel, and, at the open door, she gathered my hair together and tied it behind my neck.

"Well," I said.

She stood on tiptoes, preparing in the usual way to kiss me farewell. But then she recollected herself, backed off, and laughed in embarrassment.

I leaned forward and kissed her chastely on her forehead.

"You *will* think of it?"

"I have said."

She shut the door at that, and I set off for Ash Farm.
It was as fine an October morning as one could hope for—
the year being, let me see, yes, the year of *their* Lord 1797.
That's forty years ago almost to the day. We have a new,
young Queen on the throne now, a beauty by all reports.
But she cannot have the beauty that my own Queenie had
then, beautiful even in her misery, as I made for the coast
road. The risen sun shone from the bright blue heaven; it
sparkled off the waters of the Bristol Channel. The leaves
were turning, yellow, orange, deep red; the moors themselves blazed with color. I swung along the road in the crisp
air, my mood of dejection soon lifting. It was good to be
young and strong and alive; it was good to have courtship
and marriage in prospect. I whistled as I went. And I be-
thought me of Queenie's proposal, which with every step
away from Porlock began to seem less and less foolish, more
and more pleasing. To my shame, I entertained gross and
libidinous phantasies of having *two* young women to serve
my eager lusts, of enjoying the sensual pleasures of what
the Froggies call a *ménage à trois*. Of course, I *knew* my
thoughts to be phantastical, but I enjoyed them for all that.
They gave a spring to my step, and I thought of myself as
no end of a fine fellow. Queenie would be all right. The
problem would be solved. "There is in human nature generally more of the fool than of the wise." Thus Sir Francis,

and he adds: "Therefore those faculties by which the foolish part of men's minds is taken are most potent." Meanwhile, I descended with the road towards Ash Farm.

I was greeted very cordially at the farmhouse door by Mrs. Penry, the farmer's wife. She and I always got along well together, and from time to time I would tune her spinet for her. Tom, her factotum, was busy about farm business at the moment, she said, but would presently be free to drive me into Lynmouth. Would I care to go in while waiting and recreate myself? The weather being so fine, I said, I would prefer to take my ease out here, sitting on the rustic bench before its table. Perhaps Mrs. Penry had one of her splendid fish pies for me? And a draught of Mr. Penry's excellent ale to wash it down? Both would be mine, she assured me.

I had finished my repast and, Tom not being yet back, had called for more ale when a young man of about my own age appeared at the farmhouse door, for a moment half-in, half-out and supporting himself groggily with one hand on the lintel. Then he approached.

"Your servant, sir."

I stood up. "And yours, sir."

"Pray be seated, sir. I may join you?"

We sat on the bench together. He was a handsome enough young fellow: thick dark hair, unbound and descending to his shoulders; thick dark brows spread above large eyes he strove to keep open; a thin, long nose; plump, pouting red lips. His complexion was ruddy, but a sick pallor beneath the ruddiness sought expression. He told me his name, but at a distance of forty years I cannot recall it. And yet I see him clearly enough, as if he sat beside me now.

He was, he told me, something of a philosopher, something of a journalist, even something of a poet. Indeed, he had been engaged in poetic composition when my cry for more ale had broken in upon his thoughts. He daffed aside my apology: " 'Tis no matter." I told him of my own vocation and of what brought me to Ash Farm from Porlock.

We sat for a little while gazing about us in companionable silence. Before us stretched Culbone Combe. There bursts from beneath the little Culbone church a stream that races through a wooded gully between the hills, and so to the sea.

"See how the sun sparkles on that freshet there and turns mere water into a cascade of precious stones!"

"The source is a vast cavern beneath the church," I told him.

"How deep is it?" he asked, with eager interest.

"Its depth is known only to God; man cannot measure it."

The very notion seemed to delight him. "A cavern measureless to man," he said.

At length he asked if he might see the instrument I had brought with me. I handed it to him but begged him to have a care since it belonged, so to speak, no more to me than to him.

He admired its workmanship. "To whom, then, *does* it belong?"

"It *is* to belong to a young maiden of Bristol. I am to deliver it on the morrow."

"A dulcimer for a damsel," he said. "That's good, the alliteration is good. No, better: a damsel *with* a dulcimer. That has melody." He rubbed his eyes, and then he yawned as if to swallow the world. "Forgive me." He yawned again and, wincing, rubbed his jaw. "So fine an instrument! You are a master of your craft. Is the fortunate young lady a person of name?"

"She is not *of* name, sir, although she *has* a name. I am told she is of the freshest, the most bewitching beauty. She is a Hebrew maid. The dulcimer is a present from her father, a merchant of Bristol."

"A *Hebrew* maid? No, no, that will never do."

"Not *do,* sir?" I said, reddening, taking umbrage. "I am myself of the Hebrew persuasion."

"You mistake me quite. 'Tis the rhythm, don't you see? The meter. 'A Lao*di*cian maid,' perhaps. 'A Mace*do*nian maid'—even, you will excuse a poor poet, 'a calli*py*gian maid.' But 'a Hebrew maid'? No, no, it offends the ear." Suddenly he rose to his feet, clutching his stomach, his pallor at last overcoming his ruddiness. "You must excuse me." And he half-ran, half-tottered around the farmhouse to the privy I knew to be in the rear.

Mrs. Penry emerged to tell me that Tom was even now hitching Bright Eyes to the cart. I paid my modest reckoning. From the distant privy we heard groans. Mrs. Penry shook her head in sympathy. " 'Tis the dis-*inter*-tory," she said. "He was took short on yonder moors the other day and scarce was able to crawl here, poor lamb." She went indoors, only to appear a moment later bearing a bumper of wine. "He'll be wanting this," she said, putting it at his place on the table.

On weak legs the philosopher, journalist and poet returned and dropped back onto the bench. "Loose bowels," he said. "Squidgy tummy. 'Tis the very devil." With quavering hand he took from a pocket a stoppered vial and shook from it into his wine a prodigious quantity of drops. He drank deep. "Aaah." He leaned forward and made a cradle of his arms on the table. His head he laid sideways on the cradle and closed his eyes. "Aaah," he said again. He slept, and an innocent smile formed on his cherubic lips.

But why do I go on at length about so inconsequential a meeting? Why do I tell you of a would-be poet whose name is probably lost to history and is certainly lost to me? Because I wish to delay the purpose of my narrative, to hold off what happened to me in Bristol.

Courage, Ben. Forge ahead.

Well, Tom appeared with the cart, which I mounted. I made my farewell to Mrs. Penry and begged her to convey my respects to the sleeping poet. Young Tom drove me without incident into Lynmouth. My woods had indeed been saved from the wreck, but they were waterlogged and useless. I paid the freight but abandoned the consignment; I spent the night, as planned, at the Penrose Arms in Lynmouth. The following morning I set sail with old Ralegh for Bristol. The journey was uneventful, the sea calm. Toothless old Ralegh would slobber from time to time, "Say you not so?" "Have I not the right of it?" But since his remarks, as he kept an eye to wind and weather, grew from a dispute proceeding in his own head, I did not need to respond. In due course, he moored in Bristol, and I made my way to the home of my client.

Mr. Solomon Mendoza lived in a broad, cobbled street of fine new limestone houses. A servant girl answered my knock and, with a curtsy, took me to her master's study. My prospective father-in-law rose from the chair in which he had been reading and hurried to greet me. He was a short stout man elegantly clad in black and wearing a powdered wig. He shook my hand warmly and then stood back, his head cocked to one side, the better to view me. He seemed not displeased with what he saw. We exchanged pleasantries. He asked to see the instrument he had commissioned. While he examined it, I surveyed with my good eye the room in which we stood, and I too was not displeased with what I saw: its gracious proportions, its books, paintings, statuary, furnishings; the large windows that admitted the garden's light.

"It is a masterpiece, a veritable masterpiece!" said Mr. Mendoza. "The working of the inlay alone is beyond praise. The silver and the gold have the delicacy of lace. Come, sir, let us settle our accounts before the onset of the Sabbath." It was mid-afternoon of a Friday.

I handed him the bill I had prepared before leaving

Porlock. He merely glanced at it, quibbled not at all at the sum, hurried to his escritoire, and there scribbled out a draft on his Bristol bankers, thrusting it on me as if anxious to be rid of it. I thanked him; he was all smiles.

"You will dine with us tonight? You will honor us with your presence?"

"The honor, sir, will be mine entirely."

And as if on cue, there was a knock at the door.

"Come."

A young, a very young, woman now entered, a dream of beauty with raven tresses and attired in a blue muslin gown of the most fashionable cut. Words cannot hope to describe her. Imagine, if you can, your own ideal of freshly budding femininity and you begin to see her.

"Pardon, sir, I did not know you were engaged." The voice possessed a music not to be plucked from the dulcimer I had fashioned for her.

"No, no, you must come in. Here is a young man I would have you meet. He is to dine with us tonight." And then to me: "Mr. Cardozo, this is my lovely daughter, my Susan, my Shoshana, as lovely as her mother, my late wife, of whom she is a replica."

"Oh, la, sir!" she said to her father in dimpling confusion. "Now you mock me."

"She is, I assure you, my sole reason for living, my sole delight in life."

She stood now before me. "Your servant, sir." She curtsied, her eyes modestly abased.

"Your most obedient servant, Miss Mendoza." I bowed

low before her as she rose, and then. . . . *And then my accursed mechanical eye fell from its socket.* The hand I put out to catch it served only to hit it across the room, where its sharp, bouncing contacts with floor and wall and furniture could be clearly heard.

She looked into my face, into its empty, its angry-red socket leading to terrifying darkness, with undisguised horror, a scream escaping her lips. She turned and ran still screaming from the room. Who could blame her?

What followed I cannot precisely say—although, no doubt, it had its comical aspects: Mr. Mendoza and I on our knees searching for the lost object; Mr. Mendoza finding it beside the coal scuttle. "Here, sir. This, I believe, is yours." I do remember noting instanter that it was scratched and had sustained a small nick. Such are the utterly irrelevant but lasting images of shock. And I deduce that I must have fled that place, must have walked the darkening streets of Bristol in humiliation and despair, only to fetch up at last at The Caitiff's Arms, where I surely drank a prodigious quantity of spiritous liquors, for I awoke there fully clothed on a verminous bed on the following morning, my head a sack stuffed with pain.

🐚

I said not a word to Queenie of my Bristol adventure upon my return to Porlock, and, such was her discretion, she asked me no questions. But somehow she knew that the folly of my courtship was over, and I knew somehow that she forgave me my folly. She may even have pitied me. The rats of my betrayal had nibbled a little at her trust, and that changed in turn the way we regarded each other, but the change was slight and with familiarity became imperceptible.

The years passed, the good, the bad, and the unremarkable. I taught her to read, a daunting and at first a frustrating task, but she had a lively intelligence, and ere long she caught the knack of it; she became a reader, a prodigious reader. She would read to me of an evening before a winter fire, all manner of things but most especially the essays of Sir Francis Bacon, which, like me, she came at length to have almost by heart. I also taught her to write, an easier task, but for writing she had little use and her orthography remained uniquely her own.

In time the townspeople came to accept us, not, to be sure, as friends will welcome friends, but no longer as enemies. We were tolerated—nay, we were more than merely tolerated, for Queenie had a generous heart and a liberal hand for a neighbor in trouble. But we failed to fit the mold; we lacked respectability. What was I but a Cyclopean foreigner and Jew? And Queenie? She was neither maid nor wife nor widow, and she seemed to glory in her condition. It was her charitable endeavors that brought her to the attention of the Reverend Quintus Alcock when latterly he came to live among us. He, I would say, became our friend, and many an evening he spent at our table. And Poor Willie, who adored her, and for whom she would find small tasks about the house or in the garden, and into whose grubby hand she would put a currant bun or a mince pie, or press shiny coppers or a silver sixpence.

In time I became not *wealthy*, perhaps, as today fortunes are reckoned, but no longer concerned about money. The name of Cardozo, if of no special moment in Porlock, was a distinguished name in the world of music. I told Queenie we lived too simply. I would buy land hereabouts, build her a fine house; she should have servants, keep a carriage. "Riches are for spending," says Sir Francis. She would have none of it. "How can you think of moving, Ben? Are not our children buried at the foot of the garden?" ("The joys of parents are secret," says Sir Francis, "and so are their griefs and fears.") I caused a bench to be placed beside the little graves, and there she would sit peacefully, sometimes hours together, and in all weathers. And there she is now herself buried, and there, even now, beside the mound of her grave, Poor Willie crouches, sane enough to know he will see her no more, and he howls.

I awoke to find her cold beside me. "Wake up," I said. "The fire. My breakfast. Wake up, slugabed." But I knew she was dead.

Sir Francis no longer offers comfort. What will become of me now?

The Crossing

In July of 1879, the year of her launching, the Guion Line's S.S. *Arizona* crossed the Atlantic from Queenstown to New York in seven days, ten hours and twenty-two minutes, and thus snatched the Blue Riband from the White Star's *Britannica*. On her return she knocked more than two hours off this record, and those who paid attention to such matters gasped. In November, traveling at excessive speed through dense fog off the Newfoundland Banks, the *Arizona* rammed an iceberg head-on and telescoped her bow for a very considerable length. She managed to limp to St. John's, where she was fitted with a false wooden bow, an engineering feat that enabled her to get back to the Clyde for repairs under her own steam. Curiously, both the *Arizona* and her captain, one Samuel Brooks, gained favor from this mishap, the ship for her unsinkability and Brooks for his seamanship.

It was an era of fierce competition among the transAtlantic lines. Saloon passengers had begun to choose their ships not only for the speed and the luxuries they offered but also for the personalities and reputations—in a word, the celebrity—of the men in charge. Captain Brooks was a stout man of middling height, who, with his neatly trimmed beard and the kindly wrinkles about his eyes, had the good fortune to look very much like the Prince of Wales. The ship, with this man at the helm, seemed as solid and certain as the Empire itself. And because of Prince Edward's reputation, something of his social joie de vivre attached itself to the notion of a voyage on the *Arizona*.

When not on duty, Captain Brooks mingled freely with the passengers, delighting the ladies with his extravagant courtliness and his ever-so-slightly risqué stories and the gentlemen with his capacity for hard liquor; at ship's concerts, sine qua non of trans-Atlantic travel, he sang in a light tenor and to heavy applause music-hall songs of the day. Perhaps it was this latter talent that won him his popularity with the theatrical set. Certainly, Mme. Adelina Patti, Mme. Lillie Langtry and Mr. Henry Irving, among others, spoke admiringly of him. At any rate, he was a great favorite in the saloon, especially of the fair sex, who in 1880 voted him "the handsomest of Neptune's Atlantic sons."

Shortly before noon on December 24, 1881, the *Arizona* left her Liverpool berth, slid down the Mersey, and made for Saint George's Channel. Lowering, leaden skies and a stiff, damp breeze presaged snow for Ireland and the west of England. A few sad seagulls slowly wheeled and dipped in the ship's wake. Of the several "personages" on board, only one had a name that would meet with general recognition a century later. Oscar Wilde was en route to New York, there to deliver a lecture at Chickering Hall, which, if it proved successful, would become the first of a series on an American tour. Captain Brooks, scanning the Saloon Passengers list, was not best pleased to find that name there. The captain was a regular reader of *Punch*, his principal cultural source, and *Punch* of late had been mercilessly guying Wilde in cartoon and article as the Apostle of Aestheticism, whatever that was. Nothing wholesome or manly, to be sure. One scarcely knew what to make of a chap like that.

"Keep the blighter away from my table," he growled to his purser.

"Aye, aye, sir."

"Sir George and Lady Hardwick, eh? That 'Sebastopol' Hardwick, Whiteside?"

"Yes, sir."

"Good, good. Looked over the ladies, have you?"

"Charming a bevy as could be wished, sir."

"Ah, you dog, Whiteside, you dog. Keep the usual balance at my table. Mustn't play favorites. Give every soft heart a chance to flutter, eh what?"

"As you say, sir."

"Who's this Gladstone feller? Relative of the prime minister, d'you suppose?"

"I hardly think so. He's one of the Chosen, actually."

"A Hebrew?"

"So I understand, sir."

"What, on *my* ship?"

"That's foul in him, sir," said Whiteside, who enjoyed an ironic allusion.

"And in the saloon!"

"That's fouler. I received a note about him at the Liverpool office. He owns a great many shares in the line, I am told."

"*He* does?"

"So I'm told."

"I see, yes, ahem, quite. They'll own us all before we're done. Mark my words, Whiteside. You'll live to see it."

"I fear so, sir."

"Aye, do you fear it?" The captain too knew his *Othello*. " 'A *great* many shares,' you say? Well, *you* take care of him. Carte blanche, and so forth, within the usual limits. Put him down for *your* table. And," added the captain maliciously, "let Dr. Hitchens have a bash at him too."

The rest of the list seemed unexceptionable and excited no comment. It was time to drop the pilot.

Meanwhile, "this Gladstone feller" was the last of the passengers remaining on deck, the others having long since sensibly retreated within. He stood wrapped in his greatcoat and thick woolen muffler, the brim of his hat pulled down low over his brow, and stared into the offing. By now his feet were quite numb, his eyes were tearing, and his nose was red. David Gladstone was twenty-three, only eight years removed from *The Boy's Own Paper*, in which, had he but remembered, he would have found his present pose illustrated: "Captain Stoutheart of the HMS *Fearless* Defies the Cowardly Mutineers." He *was* aware of having struck a pose, however, and this for the benefit of a pair of bright eyes beneath a fur-trimmed bonnet watching him through the saloon windows. But he would have described it—to himself, at any rate—as distinctively Byronic, revealing, in the familiar words of Macaulay, "a man proud, moody, cynical, with defiance on his brow, and misery in his heart, a scorner of his kind, yet capable of deep and strong affection." Let us excuse him and remember his age. His age and his Age. In any case, turning as one wearied by an all too familiar scene—the waters, the sky, the gulls, the offing—but in fact concerned to discover the effect of his pose upon the watching eyes, he discovered to his embarrassed disappointment that they were gone. What could he do but sigh, stamp his feet to return circulation to them, and make his way stiff-jointedly and shamefacedly towards the warmth.

✍

In many respects David Arthur Gladstone was a very fortunate young man, especially in view of his unpromising beginnings. He had been born David Lurie to a consumptive mother and a gin-sodden father, two of the poorest of London's poor Jews. His mother succumbed to her disease when the boy was scarcely three, the father to his six months later. Malachi Lurie, an occasional drayman, succeeded in getting himself run over by his own cart and team as he led his horses from a brewer's yard. The infant was looked after for a while by a kindly ragwoman who had shared the Luries' hovel, but when her fancy man objected to the brat's presence and followed up the threat of violence with an actual blow to her left eye and a twisting behind her back of her right arm, she took David to the police, who in turn took him to the Whitechapel Asylum for Hebrew Orphans, an imposing black-granite edifice in Philpot Street, just off the Commercial Road.

At the asylum the child might have done quite well enough. It was by no means the sort of grim and heartless institution so feelingly exposed by Mr. Dickens and other reformers. There he was decently housed and fed. There he would have been taught to read and write and cipher; he would have been given the rudiments of his faith and trained in a useful trade, in due course to be sent out into the world fully equipped to find his place there. All this might have shaped his future had he not, shortly after his arrival, come to the attention of Sir Benjamin Gladstone, the asylum's founder and continuing principal benefactor.

Sir Benjamin was a man of great wealth who took his charities seriously. He had himself known poverty, and he had never forgotten its pinch. "If a man is to pull himself up by his bootstraps," he would say, "he must first have boots." The orphanage and its work mattered very much to him. Accordingly, he had from the first made it his business to visit this scene of his benevolence twice a year, in the spring and in the autumn.

On one such visit, now some seventeen years ago, Sir

Benjamin was accompanied by his wife, Lady Elena. The couple had suffered the loss of their only son to meningitis a mere eighteen months before. Arthur had been five. And from that tragic moment until the day of the visit Lady Elena, inconsolable, half-mad, had kept to her rooms. This was, in fact, her first venturing forth.

In later years, she would say that it was God Almighty who must have directed her to Philpot Street. She sat in the warden's study as if elsewhere, accepting cucumber sandwiches and tea and currant cake from the warden's wife, chatting easily of this and that, but as if in a dream in which the self observes the body going through its paces. Her eyes lacked focus; she saw without seeing. In this state she wandered through the building with her husband and Warden Zitron, commenting politely, sometimes admiringly, on whatever she was shown. It was in the nursery that she suddenly became agitated.

There, sitting around a table for a meal of milk, buttered bread, and strawberry jam, were five small children in neat linen smocks, their faces scrubbed for the occasion, their hair neatly combed. The sun streamed through the big windows. The white walls were decorated with biblical scenes in bright colors: the infant Moses in the bulrushes, the young Samson slaying the lion, Queen Esther with her foot on the bowed neck of the kneeling Haman, and so on. A nurse arose as the inspection party entered. She was a buxom young woman, who curtsied shyly and blushed.

Sir Benjamin, alarmed by his wife's agitation, put out

his hand to comfort her. She turned to him, her eyes ablaze.

"It's Arthur!" she cried. "Benjy, don't you see? It's Arthur!"

The other children stared with their mouths agape, first at Lady Elena, then at David Lurie. A little girl beside him poked him in his ribs, as if to make sure he was there. David himself squirmed and picked his nose.

"Oh, my dear!" said Sir Benjamin, and he held his mad wife to him. "The visit has been far too much for you. You should not have come. I blame myself."

She broke free. "No, Benjy, *no*! I *know* he's not Arthur, not actually. I mean he *looks* like Arthur! He's the very *image* of Arthur!"

Sir Benjamin, greatly relieved, looked carefully at the child. He saw in the serious little face no resemblance whatever to his own lost son. "Why, yes, it's quite remarkable, a very close likeness indeed."

"We can't leave him here, Benjy. We must take him with us. He's ours. We must make him ours."

"But Ellie!" spluttered Sir Benjamin, startled into a private term of endearment.

Lady Elena appealed to Warden Zitron. "He *can* come with us, can't he? He would have a good home, parents. We would love him."

Lazer Zitron was warden in title only. He taught the children Hebrew, to be sure, and how to pray. But he thought of himself as *au fond* a scholar and left the running of the institution to his wife, a thoroughly competent woman. Meanwhile, he devoted the bulk of his time to his books, from which he hoped to derive at last some explanation for the puzzling oddness of life. As it was, he felt out of his depth, not knowing whether to please his benefactor or his benefactor's wife. "It would be a very great *mitzvah*," he said. "On the other hand, Sir Benjamin has already showered his abundant goodness on him."

Lady Elena ran across the room, plucked the boy from his chair, and hugged him to her bosom. "Arthur, Arthur," she said. "Kiss your mama."

"I'm David," he said, very politely but with great assurance.

"Yes, Arthur, yes," she sobbed, laughing. "You're David, of course you're David."

And that, really, was that. David Lurie became David Arthur Gladstone.

From the Journal of David Gladstone, Esq.
24 December 1881

. . . At length we enter'd the Channel, passing on our way the S.S. Great Britain *bound for Australia. The wind blew strong and cold, but the sea was dead calm, which augurs well, I hope! One might have supposed it a vast lake rather than that treacherous current which sent Lycidas to his wat'ry bier. All day we glided swiftly through the still waters.*

Altho' I have felt some slight discomfort, I am convince'd that I have already found my sea-legs. Nonetheless, mindful of my promise to my timorous mother and obedient to the dictates of Dr. McTeague, to whose strictures she had bound me but who had pronounc'd me fit for the voyage, I determin'd to eat a light meal in my cabin. Poach'd salmon, breast of cold chicken, whipp'd custard, & an excellent Chateau-Chinon, '74. Besides, it is Christmas Eve, & as always, this season, so joyous to the gentile, casts its gloom like a wet cloak over me.

25 December 1881

The day itself began in sufficiently humdrum a way. I awoke to find our good ship berth'd at Queenstown, there to receive mail and passengers before she turn'd her course again westward. Tomkins, my steward, brought me a welcome cup of scalding, strong tea. He told me cheerily that today being at once Christmas and Sunday, doubly the Lord's day, as it were, Church of England services were to be held in the Main Lounge, at eleven o'clock promptly, sir, the prayers to be read by the ship's doctor. He was sure I would not want to miss that. I saw no reason to disabuse him, noting merely what part of the ship I was to avoid in the late morning, and wish'd him a happy Christmas, which sentiment he superfluously return'd. He added that a gala Christmas dinner was to be served in mid-afternoon, sir, steam'd pudding and all, compliments of the Captain.

Tomkins is a spry little chap with ginger moustaches & a lecherous gap betwixt his teeth, a good-hearted fellow, I am sure. He has the accent of a Londoner and was doubtless born within sound of Bow bells.

I ventur'd to suggest that, with the sea so calm, the Arizona might better her own trans-Atlantic record.

"Don't you believe it, sir. Heavy wevver ahead. Never cross at this time o' year wivout a storm or two. Will vat be all, sir?"

The Dining Room was decorated with garish seasonal tinsels. In one corner stood a small Christmas tree. I was among the first to arrive for breakfast & chose to eat alone, thinking it best to wait for Boxing Day before mingling with my fellows. I ate modestly, sensible of Tomkins' warning. Smok'd haddock, porridge, butter'd scones, & plenty of bracing tea.

The prospect of Queenstown as seen from shipboard offering nothing to delight the senses, I walk'd for a while on deck, & then, leaning against the rail & feeling quite nautical, watch'd idly and without much interest as new passengers came on board. These were for the most part Irish emigrants carrying their entire possessions with them, even the small children bent beneath the weight of their bundles. They troop'd aboard silently in the raw morning, aw'd, I suppose, by the magnitude of their undertaking, & were quickly directed aft to steerage.

On the quay below was a sudden commotion. A cabriolet had driven up at a gallop, scattering porters and causing consternation among the well-wishers gather'd at the foot of the gangplank. Shouts and curses fill'd the air. The driver tipp'd his hat impudently, as if acknowledging applause. Out of the cabriolet first stepp'd and then fell a middle-aged gentleman in the last stages of inebriation. On his back upon the filthy cobbles and in his greatcoat, his hat at a comical angle, his booted feet waving in the air, an arm hoisting and shaking an ebony cane aloft, he look'd for all the world like an overturn'd beetle. "Porter! Porter, dammit!" he cried. This mouse-squeak prov'd so negligible after so terrifying a lion's roar

*that anger gave way to laughter & an ugly scene was
avoided.*

*I turn'd away in time to see, emerging on to the
deck, that charming young lady whose eyes I had first
felt upon me even as our good ship left the Mersey for
St. George's Channel. Today, when our eyes met, I
swear she smil'd at me! But even as I took a step
towards her, she return'd whence she came, & some of
the light went from the morning.*

Far more interesting than this admittedly pretty but rather
silly young lady was the passenger away from whom she
had drawn Gladstone's attention, the passenger last seen
struggling on his back at quayside, for he was Major General
James "Gallant Jack" Barth, U.S. Cavalry, retired. He was
helped to his feet uttering many a "dammit!" by a friendly
porter, who secured his luggage, and he made his way groggily up the gangplank unnoticed by young Gladstone.

☙

Major General Barth was not ordinarily an early riser, but
he had left instructions with the desk for a wake-up call at
seven a.m. sharp, at which time he would require delivered
to his room a tumbler of rum and a chaser of hot tea. The
knock at the door, gradually increasing in loudness, eventually pierced the fog in which he was sunk. He snorted
loudly and woke.

"Seven o'clock, sir!"

"Stop banging on that confounded door!"

"I *have* stopped, sir," said an aggrieved voice.

"Wait there."

No, it was not a cheerful awakening. The debauches of the previous night had wrought in him the familiar matutinal condition: a pounding head, an inward shivering, a taste in his mouth like unto a midden, and a bladder on the point of bursting. Wearily, he heaved himself erect; wearily, he swung his legs over the side of the bed. He knew he needed desperately to piss, but for the moment he was not quite sure what to do about it. His peckerino, as he called it, peeped buoyantly forth beneath the folds of the nightgown gathered around his swollen paunch. He gazed blearily at it in some wonder, knowing himself to be completely shagged. Molly, the chambermaid who had helped him into his bed and who had discreetly departed once he had sunk into snoring slumber, had in between times given full value for the five dollars he had in winking lechery offered her. What a glorious white bum! What a wonderful hairy snatch, a veritable sporran! He had been up her lubricious cunt twice, of twice he was sure, and both times they had spent together. She had even succeeded, he would be willing to swear, in getting him to a third stand, frigging him with vigor, but what followed upon that he could no longer remember.

Bending down, and so almost losing his balance, he pulled the chamber pot out from beneath the bed and pushed it with his foot to the distance he deemed suitable, granting the pressure in his bladder, his angle of declination, and the fact that it was unnecessary to make adjustments for windage. His aim was not good.

His aim, one might say, had never been good. Gallant Jack had earned his sobriquet at Chickamauga. There, drunk one morning, as was his wont, Captain Barth was heaved upon his horse, Challenger, by a loyal lieutenant and a cursing sergeant-major. His saber was placed in his hand, and he was pointed in the direction of the battle. Challenger, encouraged by a vicious kick in the flank delivered by the sergeant-major, made off at a canter; Barth's mounted company followed. Receiving no directional cues whatever from his master, who jounced and swayed about in the saddle and waved his saber aloft more in a mindless effort to retain his seat than for any bellicose purpose, Challenger arbitrarily changed direction by forty degrees and increased his pace to a gallop. The luckless company were thus led into a Confederate ambush, where in the ensuing crossfire they were cut to pieces. Captain Barth alone escaped, brought back to his own lines by a mount that completed the last few yards of the journey with his entrails dragging behind him. Miraculously, Barth himself was unscathed.

The court-martial that should have followed upon this disaster was averted by another miracle. A war correspondent of a New York daily had from a safe distance and through binoculars observed the mad gallop and its aftermath. Privy neither to the battle intentions of the Army Command nor to the insobriety of Captain Barth, he had supposed himself witness to an American equivalent of the Charge of the Light Brigade. He telegraphed his story accordingly to his paper, and overnight James Barth became Gallant Jack, the hero of Chickamauga. The Cause was better served, the Army then reasoned, by a live hero than by a hanged scoundrel, and decided to keep its counsel.

Thus a bewildered Barth was within forty-eight hours unmanacled, cleaned up, promoted to major general, and sent with an honor guard to Washington, where President Lincoln pinned to his breast the testimony of a nation's gratitude. Within a week he had been feted in that capital and in New York, and within a month he had put together a polished version of his bold exploit that, in despite of a constant alcoholic haze, he was able to deliver with aplomb from patriotic podia throughout the North. Thereafter, he was posted to Washington, where he was put to work harmlessly shuffling papers and gathering materials for his memoirs.

Having relieved his bladder and released his peckerino, he got to his feet and staggered across the room, pausing at the mirror only long enough to wince at what he saw there. True, the semblance of a military posture could still be achieved by corsets laced year by year ever more tightly. But what could be done about his features, covered in a permanent rash of broken blood vessels, features that seemed to slip down his face like melting lard? Nowadays he spent at least one hour in the chair at various tonsorial parlors: scalding hot towels, a brutal face massage and stinging lotions were added to the daily trials of a shave and a trim. Would there be time for the morning ritual today? Arriving at the door to his room, he unlocked it and pulled it open.

A wizened little man with thin, oil-slicked hair stood

there holding Barth's boots in his hand. "Morning, sir."

"Yes," said Barth, acknowledging the fact and not the greeting.

"Your boots, sir," said the servant, stooping into the room to deposit them and then rising to the posture of a question mark. "Michael Joseph Cohan, at your service. Will that be all, sir?" He held out a hopeful hand.

"No, that's *not* all, you idiot! Cohan, you say? You a Hebrew, Cohan?"

"*No,* sir!" said the servant, shocked. "I'm a good Catholic."

"Likely, likely. Not that that's much better. Well, Cohan, where's my shitting tumbler of rum and shitting cup of hot tea?"

"Nobody told me, sir."

"Shit!"

"I'll get it now, sir."

"You bet your goddamn hairy balls you will! And while you're about it, find someone to come up here and pack my trunk. Move, you little shit, move, move!" Barth derived a certain satisfaction from the speed with which Michael Joseph Cohan departed.

The years since the conclusion of hostilities between the North and the South had not been kind to Gallant Jack. So much for a nation's gratitude! The Army wasted little time in promoting and then retiring him. His pension was piddling, hardly more than pocket money for a hero who had become accustomed not only to public adulation but to a certain standard of living, invitations to the best homes, his bills and debts vanishing into the bottomless banking accounts of the nation's first families.

At first, he had become a public lecturer, capable of attracting audiences of a decent size on the circuit. His one lecture, "With Sherman from Atlanta to the Sea," had not been harmed by the awkward fact that he had not *been* with Sherman on the latter's incendiary progress. But a lecturer needs more than a single lecture. His publishers had successfully sued for the return of an advance on his never-completed memoirs. He had, moreover, accumulated alarming gambling debts that the first families were no longer willing to cover. There had come over him a certain shabbiness, a shiftiness to his eye, a damnable weakness in his limbs. Still, he tried to "strut his stuff," and he often succeeded. His agent had at last secured bookings for him in England and Ireland, meager pickings dissipated in more high living, more gambling. At the end of his tour, he had the means to pay his passage on the *Arizona,* his Queenstown hotel bill, and very little else. He was leaving the Old World with dismaying debts and hoping to re-enter the New unnoticed by his old creditors. No wonder that in his few sober moments he was terrified!

From the Journal of David Gladstone, Esq.
25 December 1881 (Cont'd)

. . . What remain'd of the day is scarce worth the recording. As we left Queenstown we met the White Star S.S. Germanic from New York, which had made the passage in eight days. The sea began to be more

turbulent as we got well into the Atlantic. I returned to my cabin, where I have remain'd since, taking only a dish of broth & a measure of brandy for nourishment.

I now feel quite unwell.

26 December 1881

The truth of Tomkins' black prophecy is manifest. All last night and throughout the day we have been in the grip of an horrendous storm. Whatever my poor stomach contain'd it has long since voided. And yet I am wrack'd with the need to vomit forth more. My limbs grow weak, & I can take no nourishment. Meanwhile, the ship tosses & plunges upon pitiless seas, her mighty engines groan, & the very bulkheads shudder. It cannot be that we shall survive this tempest.

What folly drove me from England?

Forsan et haec olim meminisse iubavit!

The light dances before my eyes, & I can write no more.

27 December 1881

This morning, Tuesday, I awoke feeling much better, altho' v. weak.

"Is the storm over with?" I ask'd Tomkins.

"Storm, sir?" replied that worthy cheerily, whistling thro' the gap in his teeth. "Bless you, sir, I wouldn't call vat a storm. More of a blow, as you might say. Heavy seas, to be sure, sir, but storm . . . well." He handed me my tea, which in calmer waters I now felt I could keep down. "You'll be wanting to be up and about today, sir. Breathe in a little fresh air."

*He was right. In the last three days I had ex-
chang'd barely two words with any but him.*

*"How long before a landlubber gets his sea-legs,
Tomkins?"*

"In my experience, sir?"

"In your inestimable experience."

"There's some never do."

*The "heavy seas," I confess to my shame, had
driven from my mind all thought of that young lady
who had smil'd upon me. But with this morning's
relative calm she had return'd, & was present to my
inner gaze ere I had well open'd my eyes. The voyage
was almost half done, & I as yet knew nothing of her.*

*I determin'd upon a brisk walk on deck, hoping that
the sea air in its freshness might lure her to similar exercise. The sea was quite boisterous but had no ill effect
upon me. The air itself, like a Hercules, clear'd the stables
of my mind. But of the beauteous young lady there
was no sign. Going within, I wander'd in vain through
the public places, even pausing once or twice before
the Ladies' Lounge. But the door to that mysterious
Bower of Delight remain'd resolutely clos'd. . . .*

In the afternoon, after a brief nap, Gladstone felt somewhat
stronger and ventured into the main lounge, where a number of his fellow passengers were already gathered. They
were disposed in several companionable groups, some in
animated conversation, and it was apparent to Gladstone
that because of his initial scruples and subsequent indispo-
sition, he had forfeited that easy introduction to strangers
the first days aboard a steamship afford. The ship's purser
detached himself from one such group upon seeing the

young man enter and made towards him. Mr. Whiteside was a robust man with a fine military bearing and old-fashioned Prince Albert whiskers. He was scarcely older than Gladstone.

"Mr. Gladstone, sir? I'm happy to see you up and about. Mr. Chalmers in our Liverpool office asked me to look out for you. Your steward tells me you've been under the weather. I hope you're quite recovered now?"

"Quite. I look forward, in fact, to enjoying something of shipboard life."

"Indeed, yes, sir." He glanced across the room where a pair of young ladies were covertly eyeing him and giggling. "Our diversions at sea are a trifle limited, but they are undoubtedly intense."

Gladstone gulped. It was she! There she stood, blushing in her loveliness, and in the company of a creature only slightly less lovely than herself, a fitting votary—or so it seemed in his heightened imagination—to that first goddess.

Gladstone did not doubt that the two young beauties had noticed him. He would have requested an immediate introduction, but a ponderously swaying figure—swaying, that is, out of the rhythm demanded by the *Arizona*'s progress through the ocean—chose at that moment to appear beside him, clutching in one hand a tumbler of rum and reaching suddenly with the other for the purser's arm. It was Gallant Jack, the inebriated gentleman of Queenstown, who strove in vain to uncross his bloodshot eyes.

"Are you all right, General?" said Whiteside.

"Weather, waves, whatever." Gallant Jack chuckled.

"Weather, waves, whatever," he said again. "Perfectly all right, though. Stomach's unreliable. Perfectly natural, what with weather, waves, whatever." He released Whiteside's arm and downed a generous swallow from his tumbler. "Any chambermaids aboard this shitty vessel?"

"You have your steward, sir."

"Not to my taste. I'm not that sort of feller, feller. Prefer chambermaids. Got any?"

"The general has an admirable sense of humor." Whiteside sought to cover his embarrassment and ease Gladstone's. "Mr. Gladstone, allow me to introduce General Barth of the United States Army."

"Retired, feller."

"As you say, sir."

Gladstone was spared further intercourse with Gallant Jack, on whose face had appeared a look of intense discomfort.

"Stomach's fluttering again. Got the shits. Where's the nearest bog?"

"Through the doors there, sir, and across the corridor."

"Here, hold this." General Barth thrust his tumbler into Whiteside's hand, turned, and staggered at a trot for the doors.

Whiteside smoothly ignored the interruption. "Perhaps you would do me the honor of joining me at my table this evening. You will find, I'm sure, that we've brought together an interesting party."

Gladstone thanked him. "May one expect to encounter that particular young lady at table?"

Whiteside seemed puzzled.

"The young lady across the room, she of the most exceptional beauty and the russet silk gown."

"Ah, of course. Miss Emily Bevis. In fact, yes. D'you know her, sir?"

Gladstone shook his head. "Alas."

"But you desire her better acquaintance?" Whiteside winked. "She is traveling with her parents, whom you see over there." He indicated a grim-looking gentleman and his frowning wife, both garbed in black, who held tumblers of what was apparently water. They stood alone, disapproving, as if their nostrils had been affronted by some foul odor. "Then I can count on you tonight?"

Gladstone assured him that he could. "And the other young lady?"

"Ah, that is Miss Arabella Tremayne. She dines, I regret, elsewhere."

Both young beauties, Gladstone could not doubt, had an eye for him. Ah, Gladstone, you dog, you!

Gladstone's journal of his voyage has very little to tell us about the ship herself: not that she had four masts of sail and two funnels, for example; or that her gross tonnage was 5,146; or that she had a single-screw, three-cylinder compound engine with the power of 6,000 horses; or that her overall length was 465 feet and her greatest breadth 46. But then, perhaps he did not know these details, and in any case he had aspirations to poetry, and unlike some of his contemporaries, he was not moved to raptures by machines. The S.S. *Arizona* had been built quite deliberately for speed—she was the first of the liners to be called "the Atlantic Greyhound"—and as a result had sacrificed passenger and cargo space to accommodate her engines, boilers and bunkers, which occupied an abnormal proportion of the space amidships. Saloon passengers, no more than 140, were located forward of the machinery, where the *Arizona*'s excessive vibration was least offensive. The saloon alone had a length of forty feet throughout the ship's breadth. There was room for seventy second-class passengers immediately abaft of the machinery, and aft of them for up to eleven hundred in steerage. Ordinarily, however, as on Gladstone's voyage, she carried only 140 there, devoting the space thus saved to more profitable, nonhuman cargo.

For saloon passengers, certainly, the *Arizona* and her sister ships were floating palaces, but palaces in which there was precious little to do. The *Arizona* had a small library, in which were to be found the principal magazines of the day, the novels of Bulwer, Dickens and Thackeray, and the newer novels of Farjeon, Blackmore and Wilkie Collins. The more serious-minded could be entertained by biographies of Lord Nelson and Napoleon or lulled by Sedley's *Rambles of a Country Parson*. The *Arizona* published her own newspaper, the *Triton*, a single sheet hastily put together and distributed late in the afternoon of every day except Sunday. This contained ship's announcements and brief articles by interested passengers. Apart from the main lounge, or saloon, there was a smoking room on the upper deck, a music room, a ladies' lounge, and a barber shop. If weather permitted, passengers could take invigorating walks on deck, "constitutionals," as they called them, where they would examine the ocean and pronounce it, inevitably, "grand," "magnificent," or "awe-inspiring." In the evenings there were usually ship's "concerts," in which they could reveal their talents. Many of the gentlemen whiled away the time playing poker, drinking champagne or more potent spirits, and betting on the day's run of the steamer. The customary reticence of the English fell away on shipboard, and people who might have cut one another dead in London became, at least for the time of their incarceration, fast friends.

Not surprisingly, the chief attraction and principal occupation of the passengers was eating. The dining hall was carpeted with Axminster. It boasted gilded mirrors and lamps, a groined ceiling supported by silver pillars, and splendid sideboards. Its starched linen cloths gleamed, its crystal, china and silverware glittered and clinked in the ship's motion. The *Arizona*'s table was the equal of the best hotel's, offering three regular meals interspersed with several "lunches." The captain's table was, of course, the prized place at which to dine, followed by the ship's doctor's and the purser's, in that order. Occasionally, the ship's doctor was the purser's guest; occasionally, the purser was the ship's doctor's. Brooks insisted on some sort of rotation, but certain favored "personages" he kept as regulars beside him. It is worth recording, since Gladstone fails to do so, the dinner menu on the evening of Whiteside's invitation.

S.S. Arizona
Bill of Fare
27 December 1881

Soups
Turtle or Spring

Fish
Scotch Salmon and Sauce Hollandaise

Entrées
Blanquettes de Poulet aux Champignons
Filets de Boeuf à la Bordelaise
Cailles sur Canapés

Joints
Saddle of Mutton and Jelly
Beef and Yorkshire Pudding
York Ham and Champagne Sauce

Poultry
Roast Turkey and Truffles
Canard Farci à l'Orange

Vegetables
Pommes de Terre Duchesse
Asparagus • Potatoes • Parsnips

Sweets
International Pudding
Rhubarb with Custard
Strawberry Jam • Tartlets • Sandwich

Pastry
Genoese Pastry • Marlborough Pudding
Gooseberry Soufflés
Lemon Cream

Dessert
Seville Oranges • Black Hamburg Grapes
English Walnuts • Madeira Nuts • Cantaloupes
Café Noir

From the Journal of David Gladstone, Esq.
27 December 1881 (Cont'd)

*. . . For my debut I dress'd with particular care, &
consequently arriv'd a little late at table. . . .*

*Mr. Whiteside rose to make the introductions.
There were to be nine in our party, Miss Emily Bevis,
General Sir George and Lady Elizabeth Hardwick, Mr.
Oscar Wilde, a Mr. and Mrs. Elmer Tupper from a
place call'd Toledo in a place call'd Ohio, and the
American general, who had still to arrive.*

*"Gladstone, eh?" said Sir George. "Gladstone?
I'd've thought Disraeli."*

*This witticism was greeted with general laughter,
most particularly by Lady Hardwick, who has the front
teeth of a squirrel & who expresses amusement in snorts.
(In fairness, neither Mr. Whiteside nor Mr. Wilde
seemed much amus'd.) My embarrassment was keen, but
I succeeded in laughing with the rest. There was no
malice in Sir George's voice, and perhaps no meaning
in his words. It is not impossible that a Crimean hero
is a fool. I think it unlikely that he toss'd a barb that
he expected to stick. . . .*

Gladstone is certainly wrong here, perhaps deliberately
so. He was sensitive enough to insult, but no doubt wished
to soften the blow to his amour propre. The general had
learned only that morning from the captain that this Gladstone fellow was a Hebrew. That he was also a rich one
hardly improved matters. One did not dine with such fellows, except, as now, at sea. All right for chaps, perhaps,
but there were ladies present. The thin edge of the wedge

and all that. The trick was to get him to dine elsewhere. The general, in fact, was rather pleased with the witty means he had found to let the blighter know that he was not welcome.

Amusement at Gladstone's expense was interrupted by the arrival of Gallant Jack. He seemed sober enough now, clear-eyed and steady on his legs. Mr. Whiteside rose to his feet.

"Allow me to present the heroic completion of our table, General Barth, United States Army, retired."

Hardwick shot up as if from a cannon. "Not 'Gallant Jack' Barth?"

"The same."

"The world has heard of Chickamauga, sir."

"You have the advantage of me, sir."

"General Hardwick. Sebastopol."

"Not 'Sebastopol' Hardwick? Not 'Slippery George'?"

Hardwick's head was nodding so fast it was in danger of falling off. "The same."

"What luck! What deuced luck!"

"Allow me to introduce you to the table."

Whiteside sank to his place. Hardwick began the introductions. When he reached Gladstone, he paused, and then, winking ferociously, he said, "And here is young Mr. Disraeli."

"Feller over there," said Barth, pointing to Mr. Whiteside, "said his name was Gladstone."

Gladstone rose from his place. "General Harsh-Wit alludes to an earlier witticism of his. Gladstone it is."

"What did the blighter call me?" said Hardwick *sotto voce* to his wife.

"General Hardwick, dear. Your name," said his lady toothily.

Those who still stood now sat down.

At this point, Gladstone found genial intercourse impossible and he dined "elsewhere," so to speak, aware, but no more than aware, that conversation was dominated by Mr. Wilde, which released him from the need to participate. Miss Bevis, to his left, strove mightily to engage the sole attention of Mr. Whiteside to her own left, less, Gladstone supposed, to avoid him, upon whom, after all, she had smiled, than to make do, Gladstone having been thrown off his stride; General Barth sought to win the attention of Mrs. Tupper in defiance of General Hardwick, who wanted to talk to him about war; Lady Hardwick was evidently quite taken by Mr. Tupper, over whose hand she spasmodically placed her own; and so the evening advanced.

Gladstone found himself able to maintain a smile of specious good-fellowship whilst privately being entertained by the difficulties of the stewards at dinner, who had, poor chaps, to walk up and down the dining room whilst the ship was pitching and rolling. They appeared to have ascertained exactly the center of gravity, and they sloped their bodies and their gait accordingly. Inanimate objects are less skillful, and a diner was ever in danger of finding a pitcher of ice water on her skirts or his potatoes and gravy on his lap. Sir George himself, to Gladstone's delight, had a very

narrow escape, the contents of a tureen of soup barely missing him.

From the Journal of David Gladstone, Esq.
28 December 1881

Not very well today. . . .

From the *Triton*
29 December 1881

. . . Preparations for the Gala New Year's
Eve Banquet are "steaming ahead at full
speed." Nor are the entertainments of our "ordinary" evenings neglected. Miss Clarissa Courtneidge, our charming "Detectrix" of "Lights
Hidden Under Bushels," has discover'd in Steerage a troupe of Roumanian Gypsies replete
with colourful costumes, violins, zithers, bangles,
spangles and tambourines. Not even our Captain's Heart of Oak is proof against the blan-
dishments of Miss Courtneidge. In brief, the
"Romany" have his permission to ascend this
evening and "make camp" among us. They will
enliven our evening with Music, Song and
Dance. A hearty round of cheers for our excellent Miss Courtneidge!

From the Journal of David Gladstone, Esq.
29 December 1881

. . . It was foggy and disagreeable at first, & a
strong sea made the ship roll, but towards evening the

fog clear'd. I was standing alone in the fo'castle and watching the sunset when I was join'd by Mr. Wilde. He is a giant of a man, far taller than I had suppos'd, perhaps six feet and three inches in height, with hair that hangs down to his broad shoulders. One might have suppos'd him a bruiser, never a poet & aesthete. His eyes are deep blue, but in no way piercing or remarkable, & his beardless face is without shape or colour, rather like a peel'd potato. He stood beside me, silent for a moment, & evidently admiring the offing.

"Tell me, Mr. Gladstone," he said at length, "what d'you think of our captain?"

"I think nothing of him, not having met him. In his favour, it may be said that he has contriv'd thus far to keep us afloat."

"The race of Irish and the race of Hebrews are much alike in the regard of those who rule this world, irritations beneath the skin of Empire. We sue for grace by virtue of our gifts & accomplishments—I say nothing of our common humanity—and jealously we are rejected. I do not believe our captain cares for me."

I had no wish to embark upon a disputation, and so remain'd silent. Besides, I knew Mr. Wilde to be accepted into the greatest houses in the land. And so we stood for a while watching the sun sink below the western horizon.

"And the ocean, sir? Is it not grand? I confess myself much mov'd by it." He plac'd a heavy hand upon my shoulder, & gestur'd with the other at the sun's departing rays, as they blended sea & sky. "What of that?"

I little thought to have met on this voyage Mr. Oscar Wilde, whose poetry I admire, & whose aesthetic philosophy has been the occasion of much unfair & ignorant notoriety in the popular press. In London, I would, I believe, have leapt at the opportunity to make his acquaintance. There are verses of my own I would not have scorn'd to show him. But he found me now with an ineradicable desire for solitude.

> *There is society, where none intrudes,*
> *By the deep sea, & music in its roar.*

That society & music had fled with Mr. Wilde's arrival, & I long'd for their return.

"I am not exactly pleas'd with the Atlantic," I said, not troubling to disguise my ill temper. "It is not so majestic as I expected. I am disappointed."

"Disappointed?" He laugh'd, & thump'd me several times, quite uncomfortably, on the shoulder. His hand was large, & its heft an anvil. "Disappointed in the Atlantic? Capital, capital!" And still laughing he left me. . . .

Gladstone was not always so aloof. The exigencies of life aboard ship and their separate statuses as outsiders threw him and Wilde frequently into one another's company. Later that very evening he encountered Wilde in the ship's woeful library. They sat and drank together, and in the course of a mutually stimulating conversation, Gladstone told the poet of his miserable origins and of his miraculous translation into a life of privilege. Wilde confessed himself amazed and suggested that such a life became the stage more than it did the scruffy, hopeless streets of life.

"There were a hundred more astonishing stories at the orphanage," said Gladstone. "In that perspective, my own is but commonplace. There was one young fellow, a year or two older than I. I can't recall his name, but a very dour young fellow he was. He had been left and then found atop a Hebrew Bible in a rather capacious handbag in the cloak-room of Victoria Station."

"You jest."

"Not in the least. I can be more precise: the Brighton Line."

Gladstone could never understand why the most neutral of his remarks always sent Wilde off into peals of laughter.

They parted when it was time to dress for dinner.

The Gypsies had arrived before Gladstone. An old, squint-eyed woman sat in a corner behind a table on which were displayed a badly chipped crystal ball and a small board with the legend "Madame Karla Knows All." In muttered col-loquy with her stood the rest of the troupe: a short, wiry man in hobnailed boots who carried a violin and a barefoot girl of seventeen or eighteen who was scratching her thigh with a tambourine. Madame Karla and Igor, the violinist, wore head scarves and large brass earrings as marks of their authenticity; the girl, Mademoiselle Olga, an ill-fitting red blouse and a calf-length, flounced orange skirt, beneath which a torn piece of petticoat peeped. Never mind. Made-moiselle Olga, with her slim, uncorseted body, her dark complexion, and her long raven tresses, possessed a beauty that swept all criticism before it.

That evening Gladstone found himself at Dr. Hitchens's table, in the company, once more, of Mr. Wilde and Miss Bevis, whose parents sat elsewhere; in fact, with Captain Brooks. Dr. Hitchens's party included, *inter alios,* a tall American with a slim goatee, who owned something he called a "Wild West Show," complete with "genu-wine" cowboys and Indians, which, if all went well, he intended to display in the spring before the "Crowned Heads of Europe"; an aging Italian contessa who claimed, almost immediately upon introduction, to have been dandled, when a small child, upon the knee of "Milord Bee-rone," who had taken unexpected but not unwelcome advantage of her; and the comedic actor Mr. Henry Wilberforce, who was to appear in a New York production of Grainger's *Leave It to Charlie!*

Dr. Hitchens was a Scot, a stout man with a bright red face and a white beard, the very image of Chaucer's Franklin, and indeed, at the gala dinner of 25 December, he had been suitably arrayed as Father Christmas. He sat opposite Gladstone at table and was much taken by the contessa, to whom he devoted almost his entire attention. His advances seemed welcome enough, and they toasted one another throughout the meal with glass after glass of wine.

Miss Bevis proved far more agreeable to Gladstone on this occasion than before. Perhaps his own elevated mood had persuaded her that his "dumps" of the other night had been a passing phenomenon and that he was, perhaps, still worthy of her attention. She glanced several times during

the first course at the purser's table, but what she saw there
did not please her. Her young friend of the other day, Miss
Arabella Tremayne, was laughing and nodding at something
Mr. Whiteside had said. The two seemed very thick. For a
moment the eyes of the young ladies met across the room,
and in Miss Tremayne's was the light of triumph. Miss Bevis
flushed, and turned to Gladstone.

"One encounters *sur un bateau à vapeur,*" she said, "a
strange sort of society, *gens les plus étranges,* wouldn't you
agree, Mr. Gladstone? One must be careful with whom one
speaks." Not, to be sure, that she supposed *him* other than
a gentleman. *Pas du tout.* But she had learned to her sorrow
that there were actually young ladies, tolerably well con-
nected, *jeunes filles du beau monde*—and here she looked
significantly at the purser's table—who in the presence of
a naval officer's uniform conducted themselves *sans frein et
sans pudeur.*

There is no doubt that Gladstone found Miss Bevis ex-
ceedingly pretty, with her plump cheeks, her charmingly
curved lips, and her white, even teeth. She told him that
her *chers parents* were to visit distant relations, *très éloignés,*
in Boston, that she hoped to see the Niagara Falls, and that
when she returned in a month to New York she would be
staying at the Brevoort Hotel. She chattered ceaselessly,
delightfully, and with great animation, leaning often towards
Gladstone, once even placing a trembling hand on his
sleeve. Beneath the table their limbs accidentally met, but
she did not move away, and her perfumed warmth suffused
him. His condition became such that he could not have risen

from his chair without the most extreme embarrassment.

Her *chère maman* and her *cher papa,* she told him, never rose for *petit déjeuner,* and the young people agreed that, weather permitting, they might meet by chance—*qui sait?* —on deck at nine in the morning for a pre-breakfast stroll, *une promenade courte.*

All during dinner Igor wandered among the tables, a fixed smile upon his face, and scraped his violin. Behind him came Mademoiselle Olga, hopping every now and then in suggestion of a dance and striking her tambourine. It was a dismal performance. As musicians they achieved that degree of harmony suggested by Madame Karla's eyes, one of which now gazed mournfully into the crystal ball while the other contemplated the room. Fortunately, no one paid them the slightest attention. Course followed course and the wine flowed freely. The Gypsies could scarcely be heard above the ever-increasing din of table conversation.

It was while the sweets were being served that the small accident occurred. In the heavy seas through which she had been steaming all day, the *Arizona* rolled more severely than usual and sent Igor crashing into "Gallant Jack" Barth, causing that gentleman to fling the contents of his wineglass into the face of Miss Throckmorton, who as a consequence screamed. Gallant Jack, meanwhile, seeking balance, reached with his free hand for the back of Mr. Wilberforce's chair, but succeeded only in knocking the chair and its occupant backwards to the floor, himself and Igor sprawled upon them. Mademoiselle Olga, in a breathtaking flash of naked white thigh, fell atop them all.

There was momentary silence in the dining room. Miss Throckmorton's scream had had its effect. The purser was hurrying over to see if his assistance was needed, and even Dr. Hitchens, swaying somewhat, to be sure, had risen to his feet. But the group on the floor were already disentangling themselves.

Gladstone lent Mademoiselle Olga a hand. "Are you hurt?" he asked.

"No, I falls all the time. Besides, I was on top." She gave him a nervous smile. "Ta, everso."

The men were now on their feet.

"Strewth, guv," said Igor, "it was a accident, honest. I lost me balance." He was trying to dust off Gallant Jack's jacket.

"All right, all right," said Gallant Jack irritably, "get your filthy hands off me." He turned to Miss Throckmorton, who was dabbing at her face with her napkin. "My dear lady, I am truly sorry. This clumsy feller here . . ."

"No harm done, I think. Fortunately, not a drop of wine entered my mouth, the Temple, as we are pleased to say, of God's Word. No need to apologize."

"I couldn't 'elp it," said Igor. " 'Ow was I to know? Look 'ere, me violin's broke!" He held it up for Gallant Jack's inspection, but the hero of Chickamauga ignored him. He turned to Wilberforce. "It was a heirloom, a Cardozo," he said, " 'anded down from generation to generation."

"That's quite enough of that," said Wilberforce.

"But it's broke!"

"Damned impertinence!" said Wilberforce.

Mademoiselle Olga took Igor by the arm. "Come on, Dad, let's 'op it. We're not wanted 'ere."

Madame Karla, as if she had received a sign from the stars, was already gathering together her crystal ball and her board. The three departed in silence, Igor holding up his broken violin and shaking his head in disbelief.

"Thank you very much for contributing to this evening's festivities," Whiteside called after them, without even a hint of irony in his voice.

The general laughter that greeted this remark was interrupted by a loud chord struck on the piano. Miss Courtneidge, bless her, played and sang, "For they are jolly good fellows," and most of the diners sang with her. Gallant Jack and Wilberforce stood and bowed to the company, and then Gallant Jack gestured to Miss Throckmorton. She was persuaded to rise and receive a round of applause too. The genial hubbub returned.

From the Journal of David Gladstone, Esq.
29 December 1881 (Cont'd)

. . . *Following that little* contretemps, *Mrs. Bevis came to our table and took Miss Bevis from me. She was feeling somewhat poorly, she said, and hop'd that her daughter would tend her in her stateroom.*

"But Mama . . ."

"If you would be so kind, my dear," said Mrs. Bevis firmly.

Dutifully but, as I thought, reluctantly Miss Bevis prepar'd to leave. "À demain," she whisper'd to me as I held her chair. "De bonne heure."

Dear Miss Bevis! What a beauty she is! But then so in her vulgar way is Mademoiselle Olga. That perfect form, that glimpse of thigh! Ah, David, David, it is not woman alone who is fickle!

When the dinner at last approached its end and coffee was being served, Mr. Whiteside rose and tapped a wineglass for attention.

"It is, of course, the custom on land for the ladies to withdraw at this point in the proceedings and to leave the gentlemen to our port and cigars, over which we settle matters of empire and metaphysics." (Loud laughter.) "As by now you all know, however, aboard the *Arizona* that venerable—indeed, that immemorial—custom is turned on its head, and the gentlemen retire to the smoking room, where—and I speak with authority—cigars and port, among other things, may be obtained." (Laughter and cries of "Hear, hear!") "But before we depart this evening, shall we not have a little non-Romany musical entertainment?" (Laughter at the allusion to "non-Romany," thumps on the table, tapping of glasses, and cries of "Yes, yes!") "Dr. Hitchens will, I'm sure, confirm that music is a sovereign aid to good digestion."

Dr. Hitchens, who had been drinking heavily, rose from his seat, raised an arm as if about to declaim, swayed for a moment, and then sat down again. There were cheers for this performance.

"I propose," Mr. Whiteside continued, "that Captain Brooks, whose musical talents are already happily familiar to us, be persuaded to offer us a song." (A great clapping of hands, and cries of "Hear, hear!" and "Captain Brooks!")

The captain rose and made a self-deprecatory gesture, but since Miss Courtneidge was already hurrying to the piano with a sheet of music in her hand, it was apparent that this item of entertainment had been agreed upon in advance.

What followed, Gladstone found to be at once shocking, highly amusing, and, to Mr. Wilde at any rate, deliberately insulting. A steward handed the captain a lily and a poppy constructed of paper. The captain gazed at these emblems very mournfully and began with the recitative of Bunthorne's song from *Patience*:

"Am I alone,
    And unobserv'd? I am!
Then let me own
    I'm an aesthetic sham!"

There were audible gasps in the dining room, and also nervous laughter. Everyone knew that in Bunthorne the irreverent W. S. Gilbert had mocked none other than Oscar Wilde; everyone sought, as discreetly as possible, to discover Mr. Wilde's reaction. In the event, he behaved very well, leaning back with elaborate nonchalance in his chair and giving every sign of being pleasantly entertained.

Captain Brooks sang the song through to the end, producing wonderfully comical and exaggeratedly thespian gestures and facial expressions. Mr. Wilberforce was heard to say that he would be honored to appear on the boards with the captain anywhere in the world.

> "Though the Philistines may jostle,
>> You will rank as an apostle
>>> In the high aesthetic band,
> If you walk down Piccadilly
>> With a poppy or a lily
>>> In your medieval hand.
>>>> And everyone will say,
>>>>> As you walk your flow'ry way,
> 'If he's content with a vegetable love,
>> Which would certainly not suit *me*,
> Why what a most particularly pure young man
>> This pure young man must be!' "

The captain presented his paper flowers to Miss Courtneidge, who pressed them to her bosom. He thanked her for her accompaniment on the piano, thanked the company for their "patience," bowed, and sat down to thunderous applause, in which, to his credit, Mr. Wilde enthusiastically joined.

Mr. Whiteside returned to his feet. "The captain has triumphantly shown the way. Which of us dares follow?"

(Cries of "Whiteside, Whiteside!") The purser, smiling, shook his head. "Perhaps we can prevail on Mr. Wilde to enter the lists?"

Mr. Wilde rose slowly to his great height, lifting an empty glass to toast the captain. "To be able at once to steer a ship and carry a tune bespeaks a multiplicity and range of talent not to be expected of mortal man. I stand here in trembling awe of it." Here he suited his gesture to his words, and produced thereby laughter, this time at the captain's expense. "It will not be thought cowardly of me, I trust, but, rather, judicious if I refrain myself from warbling." (Cries of "Shame, shame!" and genial laughter.) "After the Lord Mayor's Show—so goes the wisdom of London—comes the dust cart. The Swan of Avon expresses the identical sentiment in a more elevated fashion: 'The words of Mercury are harsh after the songs of Apollo.' Nevertheless, whether as Mercury or the dustman, I will undertake to talk for ten minutes, disrespectfully—Mr. Whiteside may time me—on any subject the captain should propose."

There was a moment's silence.

"*Dis*-respectfully, sir?" said Captain Brooks.

"Disrespectfully."

"The Queen, sir," said the captain, with triumph in his voice.

"The Queen," said Mr. Wilde, "is no subject." And he sat down to sincere applause and hearty laughter.

☙

The festivities were by no means over with Oscar Wilde's success, but Gladstone, deprived of Miss Bevis's presence and therefore growing bored, excused himself and departed the table. As he turned into his corridor a few minutes later, he saw before him two familiar figures. Mademoiselle Olga, carrying a small bundle wrapped in a scarf or kerchief, was caught by the arm in the strong grip of Tomkins.

"Let me go, you bleeder. You're hurting me."

"Now, now, miss. You knows as well as I you're not supposed to be here."

"Let go! I'm lost, I've told you and told you."

"What's the trouble, Tomkins?"

"The young lady belongs in steerage. She's no business up here, and she knows it."

Mademoiselle Olga shot Gladstone a pitiful glance and strove in vain to free herself from Tomkins's steady grasp.

"It's all right, Tomkins, she's with me. You may unhand her."

"Ah, well, sir, to be sure." And he let her go. She rubbed her upper arm. Tomkins winked an elaborate wink. "With *you,* sir? Then that's all right." He made a show of opening the door to Gladstone's stateroom. "My pleasure, sir, second only to yours." He winked once more.

Gladstone, in fact, had had no ulterior purpose other than the succor of feminine pulchritude and, of course, the downtrodden. He was surprised, therefore, when Mademoiselle Olga entered his stateroom as if she had from the first intended no less. And he was surprised when he followed her, smiling foolishly at Tomkins, who closed the door behind them. She really *was* deucedly pretty.

Scorning the easy chair, Mademoiselle Olga made straight for his bed, where the careful Tomkins had already turned down the coverlet. She tried an experimental little bounce. Hoop-la! "Let's have a kiss and cuddle then."

Young Gladstone was not a total naïf. He had experimented more than once with the ladies of the town. But it is doubtful whether he would have pursued the offer implicit in Mademoiselle Olga's suggestion were he not already sensibly aroused by the heady perfume and insistent knee of the delectable Miss Bevis, whom he knew he would never find in the careless, abandoned pose of the female now winking shamelessly at him from his bed. With Miss Bevis he might hope for more flirtation leading to further but ultimately harmless intimacies; with Mademoiselle Olga, well . . . He joined her on the bed for a kiss and a cuddle.

She fitted into him snugly. Their kisses grew more passionate. He placed an exploratory hand on her thigh, inched up beneath her skirt. She placed her hand over his and stopped its progress. She kiss-bit his ear and whispered into it, "Oh, sir, you mustn't. Oh, I shall faint. What must you think of me? Oh, sir. Would five pounds be all right?" With her last question she moved her free hand to the straining bulge in his trousers.

"Ten pounds at least."

She lay back on the bed, her skirts up about her middle, and spread her thighs. Gladstone, his member released, mounted her. Her heels, clasping him in the small of his back, held him to her. Their copulation was ardent and mutually satisfying. He lay upon her for a little while after and then withdrew.

"Was I your first?"

"Not quite," he said.

"Well, you were my best."

He stroked her cheek.

"What's your monicker, then?"

"David Gladstone."

"Like the pry minister?"

"Yes. You're not really Roumanian, are you?"

"No, course not. Me name's not Olga neither, it's Victoria, like 'Er Majesty."

"Garn!" said Gladstone.

"Strewth!"

"Well then," he said, "on this auspicious night Court and Parliament came together."

"You are a one," she said, slapping the hand that was stroking her breast, but not so hard as to dislodge it. "This old girl came down looking for someone to entertain the nobs, and Dad says to me and Gran, 'Why not?' Acksherly, I'm a music-hall *hartiste,* I am. Me and 'im are billed as Gammidge and Gammidge. 'E plays the violin, and I sings and dances. We're a nigh-class act, acksherly, but we've been down on our luck. Anyway, Dad gets this idea about New York. 'Look at 'Arry Plum,' he says. 'Look at Jenny Trouncer. They're rolling in it today. Why not us?' So 'ere we are, in the middle of the bleeding

Hatlantic. This old girl says to Dad, 'You lot look like Gypsies.' 'We are,' says Dad, quick as a wink, 'we're from Roomynia.' 'Well,' she says, ' 'ere's yer chance for champagne. 'Ows about it?' Bloody lot of good *that* did us!" She grinned.

Gladstone kissed her.

" 'Ere," she said, "who was that bleeder Dad bumped into?"

"General Barth? He's an American."

"Not the American, the other."

"Henry Wilberforce."

She groaned. "What, the actor?"

"He's to appear in New York."

"Stone a crow," she said bitterly. "That's Dad all over. We'll never get a bloody booking now."

Suddenly she sat bolt upright, looking down at him, her eyes wide open. " 'Ave you 'ad a naccident?"

"What on earth do you mean?"

"You're missing something down there, you are."

Gladstone laughed. "It was removed years ago. It's a requirement of my faith."

"Garn, God wouldn't want that!" But she half-believed him. "It must've hurt something horrid!"

"I couldn't say. I was only eight days old."

"Poor tiny thing." She took it in her hand and gently fondled it.

"But it works all right, wouldn't you say?"

"Oh, yes, it *works* all right. Look at it, it's working now. Great oaks from little acorns grow."

Joyfully he threw himself upon her, and she opened to receive him.

"No charge for this one," she whispered in his ear. "This one's free."

Let us not cast too severe an eye upon them, gentle reader. Before the voyage was over, Miss Courtneidge would be attempting to instill *virilitas* into Jock Hitchens's flagging *membrum,* and Captain Brooks would be teaching the contessa that old sea dogs know many new tricks. To flaming youth, therefore, let virtue be as wax. . . .

From the Journal of David Gladstone, Esq.
30 December 1881

This morning at a little before nine, I began my promenade courte. *Tomkins had warn'd me of the bitter weather, & so I had dress'd as warmly as possible. The fine spray that rose all about our plunging ship settl'd in frozen droplets upon me, & before long, to the imaginative eye—had there been any foolish enough to follow my progress—I must surely have resembl'd an ambulatory Snow-man. Nevertheless, I persisted, albeit with ever-diminishing ardour.*

After his twenty-third turn on deck, Gladstone saw coming towards him, not the young lady he had every reason to expect, but her father, the Right Reverend Alexander Bevis, D.D.

"Mr. Gladstone, I believe?"

"Sir."

"We alone possess the fortitude, it seems, for such

invigorating exercise upon so inclement a day. My own little family is snug within. May I join you in your perambulations?"

"I would be honored, sir."

They took a turn or two in a silence broken only by the roar of the sea, the dull rumble of the engines, and the sound Dr. Bevis produced as he rhythmically crossed his arms and pounded his own shoulders in an effort to induce warmth. He too was rapidly covered in layers of frozen spray.

At length, he spoke. "The captain has very graciously asked me to take Divine Service tomorrow morning in the saloon. It will be the last day of 1881. We may expect that night a Saturnalia. My sermon's text is Romans 3:23, 'For all have sinned, and come short of the glory of God.' " A chuckle attempted to emerge from a face frozen in melancholy. "I think that my sermon had better be brief. May I expect to find you among the worshipers, Mr. Gladstone?"

"I am of the Hebrew faith, sir."

"Ah, to be sure," he said, with no sign of surprise. "Never mind, never mind. Our Lord himself, we are taught, was born into that ancient sect. His house, we believe, has many mansions. And now my wife and daughter await my return, no doubt with eager appetites for breakfast. I will not tell them so, but between us two I confess myself chilled to the very marrow. Good morning, Mr. Gladstone." He touched the brim of his hat and left.

His meaning was patent to Gladstone without clairvoyance. The young man cursed his own folly, sought to thrust Miss Bevis from his mind, and walked the deck striving to warm himself with thoughts of Mademoiselle Olga, or, rather, the wickedly charming Victoria Gammidge.

From the *Triton*
31 December 1881

At noon today Mr. Whiteside, our amiable and indefatigable purser, announc'd that the S.S. *Arizona* had in the previous twenty-four hours logg'd 362 nautical miles, her best run of the voyage to date. This intelligence was particularly pleasing to one gentleman in the Smoking Room, who was heard to "whoop" and "holler" his delight. Strange to relate, it was receiv'd with dismay elsewhere in that Bastion of Male Privilege, where disappointment gave vent to such terms as must fetch a blush to the cheek of Innocence. Sweet Cordiality and her gentle sister Harmony return'd, however, with the popping of champagne corks. The particularly pleas'd gentleman, we are told, toasted the healths of the dismay'd, whose own glasses were liberally charg'd and cries of "Stout fellow!" were heard.

🙖

Lost: 5, & Found: 0

Lost: 1 Hat-pin, diamond and ruby,
 Item, 1 ladies' brooch, sapphire and gold filigree;
 Item, gentlemen's cuff-links, pair, gold;

Item, gentlemen's fob-watch, gold, inscribed
"J.G.C., 1853";

Item, 1 ladies' shawl, silk, green and gold.
Anyone finding these or any other lost objects is
kindly requested to convey them to the Purser
or to any other ship's officer.

※

Overheard on Deck:

Sweet young thing, deeply puzzled: "But,
Father, what is an Aesthete?"

Father, ruminatively: "An Aesthete, my
dear, is, as it were, a Callimaniac."

S.Y.T., the light dawning: "Callow maniac?
In other words, Father, an Aesthete is an im-
mature madman?"

F., hastily: "As to that, my dear, I cannot
say."

※

By now the tedium of an Atlantic crossing had seeped like
bog mist from steerage through second class to the saloon.
The sea, however various, remained the sea, the sky the
sky. Besides, the weather was discouraging. A sudden
plunge of the bow, and the Right Honorable Harold Tavistock, M.P., a man who had at wearisome length praised
the benefits of a brisk walk after every meal, was thrown
off his feet by a niagara of icy salt water and sent skittering
some forty paces on deck. That the news of his accident
should be greeted by amusement rather than compassion

tells us something about the miasma creeping into the saloon. The diversions of shipboard had become routine; new
friendships were becoming stale. Short of a disaster, the
S.S. *Arizona* had nothing novel to offer. Everyone was now
aware that this was not to be a record-breaking crossing.
The second of January was being touted as their probable
arrival date. Those who had hoped to spend New Year's
Day in New York felt betrayed.

Only Miss Courtneidge could have wished the passage
prolonged. She had not felt quite so dazzling, so accomplished, so much the cynosure, since that glorious day in
1847 when as a mere girl she had won the archery prize at
the late Lord Godalming's garden fête in Shropshire, beating
not only the beastly Godalming children but also her own
beastly brother, Aubrey. It was no wonder, therefore, that
she threw herself so enthusiastically into the organizing of
the New Year's Eve entertainment. (According to Miss
Throckmorton, an officer in the British Temperance Union
and she whose face had had the misfortune to receive the
discharge from Gallant Jack's wineglass, organizing was not
all that Miss Courtneidge threw herself into.)

"Do you *never* sing, Mr. Gladstone, not even in the
bathtub?" Miss Courtneidge blushed a little at her boldness.

"Not even there."

"Prestidigitation, perhaps?"

"I'm afraid not."

"You can recite, I'm sure."

For a second, Gladstone was tempted. "So sorry, Miss
Courtneidge."

Dr. Hitchens's sympathetic ear was always available to her.

"Whatever am I to do, Doctor? Mr. Tavistock is incapacitated, poor dear man, and Mr. Gladstone was my last hope." She cast her sorrowful eyes upon him.

"But shewrrly, Miss Coorrtnidge, therre's morre than enoff heerr. You've achieved wonnderrs."

"You are too kind."

"If I cood be of onny help to ye . . . Clarissa?" He paused. "I tack the liberrty."

"Would you?"

"D'ye ken 'O Thou, Wha' in Ma Harrt Dost Dwell'?"

Miss Courtneidge looked away. "Oh, James," she breathed.

"Ma frrends," he said, "call me Jock."

"Oh, Jock . . ."

❧

The atmosphere in the dining hall that evening was one of determined gaiety. New buntings and clusters of balloons augmented the Christmas decorations; even the piano was draped in a colorful shawl. The passengers, as if willing to give the *Arizona* one more chance, had dressed themselves with particular care. Starched shirts shone; studs and cuff links gleamed. The ladies had donned their most gorgeous gowns and adorned themselves in their richest jewels. A steward showed Gladstone to a table far from the Misses Bevis and Tremayne, who, apparently reconciled, were giggling together beside the captain.

As the sweets were consumed and the coffee was served, Miss Courtneidge glanced at her list. The episode of the Roumanian Gypsies had created an anxiety in her that had not yet left, but, as Jock had whispered to her, the fault for that fiasco was scarcely hers. The best of the evening still lay ahead.

But Gladstone had had enough. It was not that he lacked the stomach to sit through yet another of Miss Courtneidge's "programs"—although that much was certainly true, particularly since she herself had spoken of this evening's list as "jumbo." Nor was it that he longed to return to his stateroom, where, a little before midnight, he was to be joined by the lubricious Victoria Gammidge—although that much too was certainly true. It was that Gladstone had always felt somewhat alien among his gentile countrymen, even those of that class among whom he had spent most of his life, those among whom he moved with seeming ease and freedom. There was forever something behind their hooded eyes, he felt, some unspoken thing, that locked him out. Yet through that he had learned to navigate. So long as the discreet signposts of social intercourse remained fixed in place, he negotiated quite successfully the world in which fortune had placed him. But when they began to disappear, as now, when tongues began to loosen from too much wine, when eyes began to blear or grow fever bright, when *politesse* began to sink into good-fellowship, then Gladstone began to sense his own vulnerability. He did not fear a physical attack, of course. No, what he feared was that the unspoken thing would be given utterance, that acceptance, conditional upon a conspiracy of silence, would be publicly revealed as sham. Making his excuses to his table companions, he rose and left.

☙

Supposing that after the gala of the night before his young gentleman would want a decent lie-in, Tomkins did not appear with tea until quite late in the morning. But he found Gladstone fully dressed and in high good humor, busily scribbling away in a large morocco-bound notebook.

"Ah, there you are! My tea at last! Good fellow."

"Morning, sir."

Gladstone wagged a mocking finger at him. "Something of a slugabed today, eh?"

The steward had been roused that morning, as always, at five o'clock, and since then he had been quite busy enough. We must put it down to his native decency, his sense of place, or to both that he answered entirely without rancor. "Had a nip myself, sir, me and my mates, when midnight rolled around."

"Good for you and your mates! A happy new year, Tomkins!"

"A happy new year to you too, sir."

What a jolly good chap Tomkins was! Salt of the earth, without a doubt. Or rather, he thought, smiling, salt of the sea. Yes, that was it: salt of the sea, "acksherly."

"I seem to have mislaid the cuff links I wore last night," he said, "a small pair, turquoise in gold chasing.

Do keep an eye out for them when you tidy up. They must be rolling around somewhere."

"Funny, that, sir. Mr. Wilberforce was just complaining about a silver cigar case what's turned up missing. And I hear that some of the other passengers have lost odds and ends too. Lady Hardwick can't find her Turkish pillbox. It makes you think."

It certainly made Gladstone think. He glanced at the corner where last night Victoria Gammidge had tossed her small bundle. No, of course not. It was dastardly of him to think so. But his initial silence startled Tomkins, who had expected at the very least a few sobering reflections on the mysteries of coincidence.

"No doubt they'll all reappear before long. Now, what sort of a day are we in for?"

"Better prepare yourself, sir. You're to have your storm at last."

Only then did Gladstone note the alarming pitch and roll of his cabin.

☙

Late in the afternoon of January the second, 1882, the *Arizona* passed the lighthouse at Sandy Hook, made for the Narrows, and dropped anchor at the Quarantine Station of Clifton, Staten Island. It was bitterly cold under dark, angry skies, and an icy wind blew from the northwest. A health officer boarded promptly and to loud cheers from the passengers crowding the decks, but he had a disappointing message to convey. While it was his duty to board every vessel as soon as practicable after her arrival—hence his presence—it was *not* his duty to carry out his inspection between the hours of sunset and sunrise—hence his imminent departure. He would return at first light. As the news spread on deck, there were cries of "Shame!" "Bad show!" "Oh, I say!" and some passengers began to drift back inside.

But they were now within sight of the New World and their long journey's end. One more dinner aboard the dear old *Arizona* and they would be in New York! Their excitement was irrepressible, almost giddy. And so when a small boat was spotted making towards them over the billows from the boarding station at Clifton, they rushed to the side in as festive a mood as if at a summer regatta and watched its progress. "One-two, one-two!" shouted Sir George, making a megaphone of his hands, and everyone laughed at his splendid wit. She drew alongside, and five men began the perilous ascent of the rope ladder.

"Who the dickens are you?" called down Mr. Chester A. Dabney, a member of the New York Bar, whose skill at poker had made him hated in the smoking room. "Excuse me, ladies." The ladies themselves greeted the latter remark with high hilarity.

"Reporters," one of the climbers shouted back.

"What do you want?"

"Oscar Wilde." The first reporter was now on board.

The passengers who welcomed them were utterly astonished.

"What the dickens do you want with him?" asked Dabney, not even pausing to excuse himself.

"*Mais ça c'est drôle!*" tittered Miss Tremayne, poking Miss Bevis.

"*C'est plus que drôle,*" giggled Miss Bevis, poking her in return, "*c'est incroyable!* Too too utterly *incroyable!*"

"Come inside with us and have a drink," chortled Sir George.

"And we'll tell you all about him," hooted Dabney.

But the oarsmen in the boat had specifically warned the reporters that they would wait for them for ten minutes and no more. A steward was dispatched immediately to find Wilde. . . .

Ah, there he was in the companionway, unmistakable in a fur-lined ulster of bottle green, yellow kid gloves, and a fur hat that sat like a turban on his long hair. He was talking to David Gladstone, whom they saw him slap affectionately on the shoulder.

"The Grand," he was saying.

"The Fifth Avenue," said Gladstone, and he left the poet to his fate.

The reporters pounced.

"How old are you, Oscar?" asked the man from the *Journal.*

"Twenty-six last October," said Wilde, startled by the familiarity but sufficiently in command of his wits to lop from his age two quite unnecessary years.

"What did you come to America for, Mr. Wilde?" asked the man from the *Times.*

"To lecture at Chickering Hall, and elsewhere if the public approve of my philosophy. Also to produce a play on Nihilism."

"Ah, your 'philosophy,' " said the man from the *Tribune*. "Aesthetics, right? And how would you define aesthetics?" He noted that Wilde began his reply with "a big British haw-haw."

"Aesthetics, you know, are the science of the beautiful. In this modern movement there is a search after the true, you know. Aestheticism is a sort of correlation of all the arts."

But this was not the stuff of which newspapers are sold. The men from the *Sun* and the *Herald* took their turn.

"When d'you get up in the morning?"

"I never get up in the morning—unless, as now, I'm arriving in New York."

"D'you like your eggs fried on one side or both?"

"You must ask someone who *does* get up in the morning."

"What did you think of the Atlantic?"

"The Atlantic?" said Wilde *sotto voce,* peering shortsightedly for Gladstone, who stood in fact well out of earshot staring at the black bulk of Staten Island. "The Atlantic was a disappointment to me. I found it to be less majestic than I had supposed."

Soon the reporters left Wilde to himself and wandered down the deck in search of livelier copy about him. Mr. Tavistock, M.P., his temples still wrapped in a bandage from his fall, recalled that Wilde had been quite taken by the beauty of a Roumanian Gypsy girl in steerage; he had even remarked that he sometimes wished he had been born a Gypsy. Wasn't that outrageous? Miss Throckmorton was struck by the oddness of some of his locutions. What locutions? "Well, he says such things as 'consummately soulful' and—what was that other?—oh, yes, 'superlatively aesthetic.' " "Yes," tittered Miss Tremayne, "and 'too too utterly.' " "And," giggled Miss Bevis, " 'utterly too too.' " The young ladies hugged one another in delight. Everyone laughed in recollection of these comical expressions.

Captain Brooks, however, caught descending from the bridge, was rather less than jovial: "I wish I had that man lashed to the bowsprit on the windward side."

The reporter from the *Herald* sought out Gladstone.

"Are you a particular friend of Oscar's?"

"I met Mr. Wilde for the first time on shipboard."

"What d'you think of him?"

"I think him a fine poet and a witty dinner companion."

"Yeah, sure." The interview was a dud. Still, "What's your name?"

"David Gladstone."

The reporter pricked up his ears. "Are you related to the prime minister, sir?"

Gladstone sighed. "Not in the remotest degree."

"What brings you to America?"

"To see what is to be seen."

"Are you on a mission of some kind for your government? Will you go to Washington?"

"Certainly I hope to include Washington in my tour."

But by now the oarsmen in the small boat were shouting that they would wait no longer, the sea was treacherous and they were stiff with cold. The reporters were compelled to withdraw, although reluctantly, for the passengers pursued them to the side, eager to tell them more.

Dinner on that last evening had a hectic quality to it. Most of the passengers were heartily sick of one another and as a consequence strove mightily to suggest the opposite. They exchanged itineraries and places of possible social confluence in America. They laughed, they drank, they made merry. They banqueted in Lucullan proportions. Enforced gaiety and deliberate excess was the chosen mode. Gladstone made his excuses much earlier than usual. There was none in the dining room, with the exception of Mr. Wilde, whom he expected or wished to see again.

He noticed, as he approached his stateroom, that his door was slightly ajar and that a light burned within. He supposed its occupant to be Tomkins, which would be all to the good, since he hoped to arrange for a bottle of champagne and two glasses to be brought there before Victoria Gammidge's arrival. This was to be, after all, their last erotic encounter. And so he strode cheerfully in—only to discover Major General Barth bent over the small bureau, his hand in the tooled-leather box in which Gladstone kept his studs, cuff links, pins, banknotes and other items of value. Gallant Jack looked up at him, an expression of utter horror on his face.

Gladstone's horror was perhaps as great as Gallant Jack's, but of the two Gladstone's position was unassailable. "An unexpected pleasure, General," he said.

"Mistook the cabin. They all look much the same. Understandable error."

"And that box there, the one in which your hand still lingers, the one emblazoned with the initials D.G., is that too to be found in every cabin?"

Slowly, Gallant Jack removed his hand from the box; slowly, he reached into his pockets and scattered from them onto the bureau various shiny objects. "You will recognize those that are your own." He hung his head in evident misery, in evident shame, in evident fear of the consequences.

"But why, General?"

Gallant Jack staggered to the bunk, fell upon it, sat with his head in his hands, sobbed.

"Old soldier, sir. Put my life on the line. Gave my all. Involved in heroic action the world is all too willing to forget. Put out to pasture, sir, while still in my prime. Ungrateful country, shitting politicians, shitting timeservers. Pension a joke. Penniless, penniless." He groaned, sought to rise, but fell back. He looked up at Gladstone, his eyes bloodshot, his features indistinct. "Had too much rum, thought I saw a solution. Demon rum, you know." His shoulders heaved as he began once more to sob. "That it should come to this!" He took from his sleeve one of Gladstone's silk handkerchiefs and blew his nose violently into it. "Owe money on both sides of the Atlantic, lots of it, can't pay. Shitting Jews into me for thousands. Once you start down that road, well . . . Doors once open, the best houses, shut in my face. Best houses, I tell you. Four hundred. Terrible, terrible. Once a man, now a blubbering heap, as you see." He blubbered, demonstratively. "Have to sneak off the shitting boat tomorrow. They'll be lying in wait for me. Creditors, I mean. God knows where I'll lay my head tomorrow night. Perhaps in jail, up to you. Penniless." He looked up at Gladstone now with eyes more sharply focused. "What will you do?"

What indeed? Gladstone picked from the scattering on the bureau the items that were his and put them back in their box. "The rest must be returned to their owners. No other course is possible."

"But how? Short of confessing. The shame eats at my vitals; it burns. A hero once, y'know. All that now forgotten."

"Here's a possibility," said Gladstone. "Take these, and whatever other, stolen items to the purser. Say that by chance you apprehended the thief. Say that he was a gentleman. Say, moreover, that honor forbids you to mention his name. He is contrite and will not undertake such a desperate course again. Say you trust his word. The items are to be returned to their owners, items once lost and now found. Do this, and I shall say nothing more of what has occurred here. Do less than this and I must speak."

Gallant Jack rose to his feet still sobbing. "Oh, sir, you are too kind. I shall do as you say. I shall follow your advice to the letter." But there was in his weeping eyes a look of cunning. He rubbed his hands together. "You have saved me from one at least of my appalling fates. From the others you may stand aloof."

Gladstone, conscious of having behaved admirably, wished to play his trump card. He took from his treasure box what Gallant Jack's eager hand had not yet reached when apprehended: a thick wad of banknotes. From it he peeled fifty pounds. "Take this," he said. "You will find where to lay your head."

"Oh, sir, I cannot, for my honor."

"Your *honor*, sir?"

"You do right to rebuke me." He stuffed the banknotes into his shirt.

There was a knock at the door. Gallant Jack swept what was left of the shiny objects on the bureau into his pockets.

"Come," said Gladstone.

Into his stateroom came Victoria Gammidge, a little put out to discover Gladstone had a visitor. "Oh!" she said.

"I'm on the point of leaving," said Gallant Jack, but his face was transformed by a leer.

"We know what to do, then?" said Gladstone enigmatically.

"We know, sir," said Gallant Jack, still leering. He glanced at the handkerchief tied into a small bundle that Victoria Gammidge carried in her hand, his eyes sharpening with malicious understanding.

In flounced Miss Gammidge; out slouched Gallant Jack.

"I don't like 'im," said Victoria.

"You should not like him," said Gladstone.

Over what followed we draw a modest veil.

From the New York Sun
3 January 1882
A Wild(e) Lament

No longer can th' Atlantic Sea
Pretend to any majesty:
It seems the mighty billows' rage
Was too too tame for our new sage.
Let shame upon the deep be piled
For disappointing Oscar Wilde.

From the New York Herald
3 January 1882
A Scientist of the Beautiful
Arrives in New York

. . . Also on board was Mr. David Gladstone, a nephew of the British Prime Minister. Mr. Gladstone vigorously denied that his mission in America is either official or clandestine. He confessed, however, that he intends to visit our nation's capital. . . .

The health officer was as good as his word, arriving in the first light of a brilliant, cloudless dawn. His inspection took no more than twenty minutes. Those who had risen early on this their last day on board stood blinking in the brightness that danced off the waves and the floating chunks of ice. They watched as more than five hundred mailbags were discharged into a tiny wooden white steamer, gaily decorated with the Stars and Stripes, that bobbed alongside. The health officer and the mailboat left at the same time, although in opposite directions. Despite the wash of the sunlight, it was still bitterly cold. On the thermometer outside the smoking room the mercury stood at ten degrees.

The *Arizona* now began her halting progress through the Upper Bay, stopping almost as soon as she had started to take aboard two officers of the custom house. These gentlemen, "as if by custom," immediately set themselves up at the captain's table in the saloon and, fortified with steaming mugs of coffee and brandy, prepared to take declarations.

When the ship stopped for the second time, Gladstone was back in his cabin completing with Tomkins's help the final stages of his packing.

"What the devil is it this time?"

"Ah, that'll be the private yacht for them wiv gummint connections, sir. They were first through customs."

Gladstone was mildly interested, enough to leave Tomkins to it and climb to the deck. The small steamer-yacht was already departing the side. As he turned his head from the yacht to the offing, he saw a sight of breathtaking beauty. Beyond the dancing waves he saw in a single *coup d'oeil* three cities glittering magically in the sunlight. Nothing had prepared him for the grandeur of that sight. Before him New York, to the right Brooklyn, to the left Jersey City. At that distance the buildings, no mere aggregations of houses, seemed minuscule, and yet some must have reached as high as ten storeys; church spires dotted these cities, and thousands upon thousands of tiny tendrils of white smoke rose and vanished into the clear blue skies. There was the North River, the mouth of the Hudson, there the East River, over which, plainly visible, a gigantic bridge neared completion, eventually to join Brooklyn and New York. Countless the craft plying these rivers between shores bristling with wharves and piers. Here was a grandeur of a scale, thought Gladstone, that befitted a great continent.

When the *Arizona* stopped for the third time, it was to transfer the immigrants to Castle Garden. Victoria Gammidge, her father and her grandmother stood on the crowded deck of the Guion tender, Victoria craning her neck to see, beyond the looming bulk of the steamship, the faces of the saloon passengers, who leaned over the railing in mild interest. David Gladstone was not among them. Her teeth were chattering, for her coat was pitiably thin and she had no gloves. Her father and grandmother— that is to say, Igor and Madame Karla—were scarcely better clad or more comfortable. Each of them had an escort; each of them had an arm firmly held by a burly New York policeman. Victoria sniffed, shrugged, and turned her back on the *Arizona*.

At that moment, in fact, Gladstone was facing the custom-house officers in the saloon. The senior officer, a genial old man with snowy hair, asked the questions; his subordinate, younger and sharp-faced, took down the an-swers with a stubby indelible pencil that from time to time he licked with an empurpled tongue. Gladstone was asked first for his name and addresses and then for an inventory of his baggage.

"Occupation?"

"Gentleman."

The sharp-faced subordinate snickered. "Unem-ployed," he translated, licking his pencil before writing that word on the declaration form.

"Then I shall have to ask you for your credit references. A formality, no more." The senior customs officer spoke in the kindly tones of a schoolmaster coaxing an answer from a willing but dim-witted pupil.

"House of Gladstone, Threadneedle Street, London; Glattstein and Company, Nassau Street, New York." The senior officer turned with a look of the surprise to the *Arizona*'s purser, standing in readiness to help his passengers, should his help be needed. Mr. Whiteside nodded.

"Is something wrong?" asked Gladstone.

"Nothing, not a thing in the world. And now . . ."

Gladstone was asked whether he had anything dutiable to declare and required to take an oath as to the truth of all he had said. These formalities completed and his depo-sitions signed, the snickering subordinate handed him a yel-low ticket.

"Next," said the senior officer warmly to Miss Court-neidge, who sat behind Gladstone, pale in anticipation of her ordeal.

Gladstone wanted fresh air, no matter how bitterly cold, and so went on deck. He lighted a slim cigar and gazed idly down at the Guion tender and its load of immigrants.

"They're under arrest, all three of 'em," said Mr. Dabney, who stood beside him, leaning on the rail.

"Who are?" said Gladstone.

"Them," said Mr. Dabney, pointing. "The Gypsies. You remember, the dining room? Throwing wine in Miss Throckmorton's face? Assaulting the general and Mr. Wilberforce?"

Far below Gladstone saw the miserable huddle of Gammidges and their uniformed escort. "They've not been arrested for that, surely? It was an accident! I saw it!"

"An accident? Maybe yes, maybe no. Maybe just a ruse to cover a little pocket-picking. The point is, they were found with the 'lost' items in their possession. *Prima facie,* you can bet on it. Common thieves, every one of them." He turned comfortably in place and rubbed his back on the rail. "Well, sir, we've got the general to thank for their arrest. Not much you can get past the eye of an American soldier: you can bet on that, too." He nodded further along the deck. "There he is now."

Gladstone saw a group made up of Captain Brooks, Major General Barth, a police sergeant, and Tomkins, who stood at a slight, deferential distance. The police sergeant shook Gallant Jack by the hand, saluted the Captain, and nodded at Tomkins. Then he turned and went over the side to join the tender. Captain Brooks and Gallant Jack went off together; Tomkins went below. Throwing a hasty fare-well over his shoulder to Dabney, Gladstone hurried after his steward.

"General *Barth* turned them in?"

"Yes, sir. Said he had his suspicions."

"The hypocritical blackguard!"

"Now, now, sir. I know you were sweet on the young lady. She's quite an eyeful, if I may make so bold. But they were found with the goods on them. Thieving's thieving. There's no excusing it, begging your pardon."

"*All* the stolen items were found in their possession?"

"Not, as you might say, *all*. But most, sir. Some may have been lost in the ordinary way. We're still searching. Just think, sir: if the true thieves hadn't been caught, sus-picion would have fallen on the crew, especially on the stewards. It's only natural, however unfair. Our very lives depend upon trust, sir. You *must* trust us, or where are we? Or you, sir? No, they were caught dead to rights." He looked apologetically at Gladstone. "The young lady had found a means of getting into the saloon, sir, a place where she had no business to be. I didn't tell Captain Brooks all I might've. Gentlemen will have their fun, and you are one of *my* gentlemen. As a rule, where's the harm in it?" He lowered his eyes in embarrassment. "She had your missing cuff links on her, sir, more's the pity."

"Don't fret, old fellow. You have the right of it. My quarrel is not with you. You have served me faithfully and well, and I trust I shall encounter you again. I am, in a sense, doubly your employer: as passenger and as one whose family has some financial interest in the line. Rest assured that my report home will ring loud with the praises of a certain Tomkins. Meanwhile . . ." Gladstone removed from a pocket the generous tip he had prepared for his steward and handed it to him. "Let this be an earnest of my gratitude."

"Oh, thank you, sir!" Tomkins beamed. "No offense meant, sir."

"No offense taken."

And, indeed, he *had* no quarrel with his steward. Gladstone was a representative of his class and his time. It was not so long ago that petty thieves had been transported for life, not so long before that that they had been hanged. He could scarcely remember his life before the orphanage. Property was sacred, and the need for its retention and augmentation was propelled by an almost mystical imperative. He had enjoyed Victoria Gammidge, enjoyed not merely her body but also her person, her personhood. She, he believed, had taken pleasure, not merely physical pleasure, in their union. But she had cost him ten pounds a night, and he did not doubt that she would have willingly pleasured any man on board for ten pounds a night. The thought that she might be a thief had, after all, crossed his mind when Tomkins had first told him of mysterious losses aboard, but his own vanity would not then accept that she might have stolen from him. Theft appalled him, and he was content that she and her family should be punished for it. What rankled, what angered him beyond endurance— so much so that it had burst out before his steward—was injustice. Why should the Gammidges pay, as they should, for their crime while General Barth went free? The unfairness of it ate at him. He was perhaps, in advance of arrival, already in part an American. If the general could steal and get away with it, why not the Gammidges? The blackguard had made certain promises he obviously had no intention of keeping.

Gladstone knocked on the door of General Barth's cabin and walked in without waiting for a response. He found the general sitting on his trunk, a tumbler of rum in one hand, an almost empty bottle in the other. Gallant Jack's drooping features assembled themselves into something like a grin; he winked at Gladstone and raised his tumbler in a mock toast.

"General, we have unfinished business."

Gallant Jack belched. "Piss off," he said, not unkindly.

"You turned the Gammidges in for theft."

"Had to. Public duty." He grinned again.

"Has public duty prompted you to turn yourself in?"

Gallant Jack rose to his feet. His eyes had gained in focus and his color was suddenly high. "What the fuck do you mean, you little shit?"

"You know very well what I mean. I caught you in my cabin with my property on your person. Why, your very hand was in my studs box. We had an understanding—"

"Well, understand this, shit-face: you utter these bollocsing lies in the presence of any other person and I'll sue you for slander from here to fucking kingdom come. You may be sitting on a pile of shitting Jew-gold right now, but by the time I'm through with you, you'll be begging for a fucking handout. Now get out of here!" Gallant Jack swayed where he stood, the veins in his temples bulging.

Gladstone, seething in fury himself, turned on his heel and left without another word. He went directly to the purser's office and demanded an immediate interview with the Captain.

"Captain Brooks," said Whiteside, "is at his busiest now. I rather doubt I can interrupt him."

"Remind him of my connection to the line. Tell him I would not disturb him for the world were not this a matter of considerable urgency—nay, of the *greatest* urgency. He is asked to grant me the favor of five minutes. I must see him before we dock." And when Whiteside hesitated: "Go, man, now!"

Captain Brooks's face bore none of its usual benignity before passengers. He glowered. "What is this urgency, Mr. Gladstone? For the safety of the ship, I dare not leave the bridge. I suspect that the damned pilot they've sent me is drunk."

"Then I shall not delay you long. In brief, we have a thief on board."

"The thieves have been caught. They are already in custody at Castle Garden. For all this, we are in the debt of General Barth."

"General Barth is a scoundrel, sir. *He* is the thief I mean."

Captain Brooks burst into laughter. "Forgive me, but that's preposterous! General Barth a thief? What next? They went quietly, you know. No fuss. We found numerous stolen trinkets in their possession. 'It's a fair cop,' Gammidge said."

"They may well be thieves. I do not argue with that. But I caught General Barth in my cabin, his hand in one of my boxes. He may not himself have said 'It's a fair cop,' but he implied as much."

Captain Brooks looked grave. "You should know, Mr. Gladstone, that the general has told me of your response when first he spoke to you of his suspicions. He had noted your—shall we call it 'friendship'?—with the girl Gammidge and thought to warn you. You told him to mind his own business and to keep his suspicions to himself. He was much hurt by your rudeness, but put it down to the ardor of youth and your, er, *unconventional* manners."

"He is not only a thief; he is also a liar."

"You deny a relationship with that girl?" The Captain all but sneered. "As for General Barth, tell me, have you any witnesses who might support your accusation?"

Gladstone hesitated.

"In short, you have not."

"My eyes are my witnesses, the clear image in my mind of what took place. Search his luggage, for heaven's sake! There you will find witnesses in overplus."

"That I will never do! What, invade the privacy of a gentleman, search the luggage of an officer, on the mere, unsupported accusation of a . . . of a . . . er, of another gentleman?"

"You showed no such delicacy of feeling with regard

to the unfortunate Gammidges. Barth *is* no gentleman. At best, he is a blackguard. I tell you he is a thief. He has, moreover, unsatisfied creditors on both sides of the Atlantic."

Captain Brooks did not trouble to disguise his distaste. "I am persuaded that for reasons best known to yourself you have undertaken to besmirch the reputation of General Barth. I must tell you that I shall not proceed in this matter."

"You choose, in other words, to believe him rather than me?"

"It is not a matter of choice. Without incontrovertible evidence in support of your claim, I *can* do nothing."

"*Will* do nothing. You will not search his baggage. Very well, what steps do you advise me to take?"

"You will do what you must do. Once ashore, you may take your story to the police. I would advise against it. They, too, will want evidence. I know of your family's interest in the line. You will understand that my decision cannot be affected by concern over earning their displeasure. In America, General Barth is a national hero—and not here alone: the world itself pays tribute to his heroism at Chickamauga. Take care, Mr. Gladstone. And now I must go. I pray I am not too late."

❧

Captain Brooks, alas, *was* too late. The fourth stop of the *Arizona* was unscheduled. The ship suddenly stuck in the mud, and before she was freed she was boarded by more reporters in search of the Apostle of Aestheticism. They found him in the smoking room and quizzed him for the better part of an hour.

Wilde then escaped, leaving them to interviews else-where, and came upon Gladstone pacing the deck. "I do not hold out much hope for America," said Wilde. "D'you know, I was actually asked whether, were I to grow a beard, I should wear it, when I slept, above the bedclothes or beneath? 'Beneath,' I said, 'for it is beneath the sheets that pleasure commences.' They found that answer pro-found, although had they asked me what was the relation-ship between a beard and pleasure, I would have been unable to say." He noted Gladstone's vain attempt to smile.

Wilde went on, "I overheard your altercation with the Captain. No, not over*heard*, for I was too far away for that. But I observed his manner to you. Over*saw* it, perhaps. Brooks, it is clear, cares no more for you than for me. Society will always win, Mr. Gladstone. We offend it at our peril. It will close ranks and prove impregnable to the stoutest assaults of reason and justice. Do not kick against the pricks." He smiled, as at a private joke, and turned to go. "Remember, we are to meet in New York." He patted Gladstone warmly on the shoulder and left.

Gladstone, still walking alone on deck, now saw coming towards him General Sir George Hardwick and General "Gallant Jack" Barth. They were deep in conversation, per-haps comparing conditions at Sebastopol and Chickamauga. As they drew abreast, Sir George, looking icily at Glad-stone, said, "Ah, Mr. Disraeli," and he put a casual hand to his fur hat. Gallant Jack noted Gladstone with dead eyes that turned away.

Gladstone's frustration was intense. He bit his lip so fiercely he drew blood. But Wilde was right, of course—as were, finally, Captain Brooks and Gallant Jack. There was nothing to be done. The New World, so bright and glistening in the pure and frigid air, so inviting at the birth of a new year, offered no solace, no alleviation.

On the eleventh calendar day after her Liverpool departure, the S.S. *Arizona* was safe in her berth at the foot of King Street in New York. Gladstone descended.

The Affair

Bruno Sorge was lying on Olga's bed in the gloom, his arms behind his head, his ankles crossed, watching a fly on the ceiling. He had taken off his shirt as a gesture of submission to the afternoon heat and unzipped his trousers in anticipation of the lower-intestinal flatulence a simple luncheon of sliced onion on thickly buttered, seeded rye nowadays caused him. But he had not, after deliberation, removed his shoes, which, as Olga had warned him they would, had already blackened the heavy lace counterpane her parents had brought, along with the then adolescent Olga, via Rome and Buenos Aires to New York from the Old Country—that is to say, from Hungary. It was a family heirloom, a relic.

The dark green blind was drawn over the open window. Every now and then a sluggish puff of wind would shift it and admit sudden harsh summer light into the room. When this happened, the fly on the ceiling would walk a few paces, as if reminded of some urgent business, and then lapse once more into inactivity. Bruno found the always unexpected scrape of the shifting blind an oddly pleasing irritant. He watched the fly. Scrape; light. The fly strutted its stuff.

But if the fly seemed to occupy Bruno's attention, it was, so to speak, only the outer eye that followed its peregrinations closely. The inner eye was otherwise engaged. It was reviewing his career and attempting a peek into his future. For Bruno did not have much to do at the moment. His work was seasonal, his summers free. For years he had been a regular, nonchoral supernumerary in the smaller opera companies of the city, the d'Avanzo, the Second Avenue Diva, the Village Buffa and so on. But last season his career had taken an unexpected turn for the better. He now had name parts. At the Diva he had played Roberti in *Tosca*, mute, but important: the opera could scarcely have gone forward without him. At the Buffa he had played Vespone in *La Serva Padrona*, mute again, but a role whose comic potential he had realized so well that Guido Krauskopf, the visionary manager and director, had insisted he try out for Frosch in *Die Fledermaus*. His performance as the drunken turnkey had been a triumph. His friend Duncan Greenglass had sent his music critic down for opening night. The review in that week's *Village Culture* had devoted a glowing paragraph to Bruno alone: "To the role of Frosch, Bruno Sorge brings a comic gift so impressive that it reveals him as the natural heir to Chaplin, and an awareness of the sorrow lurking in the heart of hilarity that is the special wisdom of the world's great clowns. Expect to see much more of this considerable talent." The world of Greenwich

Village opera is small; the word had gotten around. Bruno could now command speaking roles. Over at the d'Avanzo, Zvi Elsasser had cast him as Selim Pasha in *The Abduction from the Seraglio* and as Samiel in *Der Freischütz*.

Bruno had bought a new suit and taken Elvira Königsberger, the aging diva of the Buffa, to lunch at Tavistock's, which, as everyone knows, is where Caruso himself had dined on alternate Thursdays. There, amid the heavy crystal and crisp napery, he had been noted. Elsasser, alarmed, had offered him a full-fledged membership in his company; Krauskopf had immediately countered with a similar offer but a larger salary. The nameless legion of supernumeraries, his former peers, fluttered about him in flattering deference. Perhaps his comet, soaring into the night, could illuminate their own lives. Duncan had urged him to acquire an agent, a navigator, so to speak, to broader horizons, to new worlds for conquest.

But after his initial elation Bruno began to be upset by his success. He had always enjoyed his anonymity, curling up safely, unnoticed, within it. Now he had great expectations, new responsibilities. The pace of his life had quickened. The world was making demands of him. And so he had begun to talk of taking a sabbatical, a season or two off, perhaps at last to write his book on the Dreyfus Affair. Yes, why not? He needed breathing space. At forty, it was time to re-examine his options.

The Affair was Bruno's avocation, his hobby. It was an interest that had begun half a lifetime ago when, as an undergraduate at Columbia College, he had taken a course in late-nineteenth-century French history. But why so prolonged a passionate interest in Dreyfus? Bruno couldn't say. An elective affinity perhaps. Like Bruno on stage and in life, Dreyfus too was a sort of supernumerary, a man not acting but acted upon. Or so it sometimes seemed to Bruno. Meanwhile, he had accumulated a vast hoard of notes. He had even written a general essay on the Affair and the chapter outline of a full-length study, which he had submitted to Duncan some months before for comment and advice.

But it was Olga, she who had once taken such pride in his association with the "Arts," who had helped him reassert perspective. "Let's not lose our heads," she had advised him. "Let's remember who's swimming around in this pond where you're suddenly the big fish. We're not talking about the Met here. This is not Covent Garden or La Scala. One hundred and fifty paying customers is a full house. We're talking about a bunch of has-beens and never-to-bes. We're talking about a man who's not even a singer. Opera, they tell me, has something to do with singing, maybe I'm mistaken, correct me. Never mind a sabbatical, my hero. Twenty-five thousand, even if you get it, no guarantees, won't get us onto Park Avenue. Just be happy you've got a job." And then, spitefully: "Your precious Elvira looked more like Carmen Miranda than Rosalinda, let alone a Hungarian countess." Arms raised and fingers snapping, a horrid fixed smile on her lips, Olga had swayed into a rhumba. "Ai-ai, ai-ai, how voot you like to go to Habana?"

She was right, of course, and not just about poor Elvira. This was no time to throw away even his minor triumph.

As quickly as he had been recognized, he would be forgotten. Others were waiting in the wings to take his place. What then? He would play Elsasser against Krauskopf. But first he would see Krauskopf, who had asked him to come in for a chat—"Soon, Bruno, come soon. I've got an idea, such an idea, it's tailor-made for *you,* tailor-made. You turn it down, you gotta be meshugga, and I'm talking meshugga. Forget Elsasser. Between you and me, the company's in deep financial shit. I say nothing about the fire laws: they had the marshals in yesterday. But not a word. I wouldn't want to do Elsasser an injury, the shmuck. Only, don't fuck around, Bruno. Come and see me soon. What I've got in mind, it could mean a whole new you." A whole new Bruno? Well, why not? Perhaps the Buffa would prove to be the petri dish, so to speak, in which he would re-create himself. But that pleasing prospect brought his thoughts back again to Olga.

At this hour and on a weekday Olga Khachaturian was at work, or, as she herself would have put it, "professionally engaged." She was, she said, an archival researcher. And, after a fashion, so she was. She researched brand names. American business clamored at the doors of Lustig Brands Research, Inc. Brand names were sacred. It was surely no accident that the firm was located in the Woolworth Building, the Cathedral of Commerce itself. Who would be so foolhardy as to launch a new product without first discovering if its brand name was also new? That way lay lawsuits. Thus Lustig Brands Research thrived, and with it Olga, who delved with enthusiasm. She was highly thought of by Saul Lustig, her boss, or, as Olga herself would say, her "senior associate." Lustig had been after Olga for years, everyone knew that. Bruno was lucky, she frequently told him, to have her.

At thirty-five Olga was ripe and beautiful. That much must be said for her. And yet for his part Bruno could not understand how he came still to be living with her. He had met her five years before in City Hall Park, whither, a juror, he had gone to pass the lunchtime court recess. A fat man sat between them on the bench reading a racing form. When he got up to leave, they both expanded into the newly available space and gave a single, audible sigh. They looked at one another and smiled. Then they began to talk: the park, the heat, the crowds, the fat man with the racing form. "My name is Olga," she told him, "but they call me Mimi." He looked sideways at her, prepared to grin. Was she having him on? But no, it was clear she meant it. "I'll call you Olga," he said.

Along with his fellows, Bruno had been warned by the judge not to discuss the case with anyone; he told Olga all about it. As for her, this was her first week with Lustig Brands Research; she thought it was a "professional engagement" with a future. The hour passed pleasantly. She shared her lunch with him; he bought them drinks from a park vendor. They agreed to meet in the evening for dinner.

That night he took her home and bedded her. To his surprise she was a virgin. The surprise was due less to the fact of her virginity at age thirty than to the skill she manifested though virginal. It was her thrust on him that tore the stubborn hymen, a wild exultant frenzy. They went for lunch every day for the balance of his term as juror and slept together more often than not.

Meanwhile the lease on his Village apartment had been running out. The building was to become a cooperative. He had the option to buy in or move out. The notion of putting down roots, even to the limited extent of purchasing an apartment, distressed him. Besides, he lacked the money. Olga suggested he move in with her. It had seemed a good idea at the time. It would solve the immediate problem and allow him to find his own place at leisure.

It had been a mistake, although they had gotten on well at first. Religious issues had never proved a cause of friction between them, not really. True, Olga was rather more a believing Catholic than he was an observant Jew, but so what? True, when he had moved in with her, she had had to take down the cross from the wall above her bed. But again, so what? She had easily adjusted to that, hadn't she? And as members of persecuted minorities, both enjoyed, if that was the word, certain similar historical memories. Her reaction to the word "Turk," for example, was much like his reaction to the word "Nazi." Besides, she was unlike any other woman he knew, which had been in itself refreshing. As for her, she had thought him eccentric and bohemian, his seeming oddness exciting, part of the gay adventure of living in Manhattan alone. She was soon disabused.

Bruno found Olga superficial. It was not that she lacked depths. It was that she lived on the surface, and the surface must be clean and bright and happy. She was deliberately unaware. Bruno kept cluttering the surface; Olga kept wiping it clean. Their illicit relationship was part of the clutter. She wanted him to marry her, the bohemian life having soon lost its allure in the conflict with her native bourgeois convictions. But Bruno sneered or shrugged or turned the conversation.

How was it possible that they were still together? Inertia was too simple an answer. Modestly he acknowledged his own blame: he did not know how to bring the affair to an end. One could not simply reject another human being, a woman whose only fault was to be openly and sincerely herself. One did not cruelly turn one's back on her after she had given him, as Olga frequently pointed out, her prime years, had surrendered herself to him like a heart quivering on an Incan altar. It was unthinkable that the gift be callously disdained. And how else if not callously, since callous it must inevitably seem?

Bruno sighed.

Scrape; light. The fly took a walk.

He got off the bed, instinctively zipping his trousers, and made for the window. He pulled the blind up and leaned out.

Olga had a second-floor apartment in a gray-painted brownstone on East Eighty-second Street. Her bedroom window faced the rectory of Saint Stephen of Hungary. Next to the rectory, in the direction of First Avenue, stood the church itself, and beyond that the church parking lot, its gates open. Bruno knew the parking lot well enough. In the rear was a shrine to which Olga would sometimes flee when he became too much for her. In the front of the shrine was a small stone bench where she would sit and rock herself calm again, reading and rereading the message behind the figure of the Virgin: "For peace people must say the rosary." They made an odd grouping, the Virgin with the face of Theda Bara rising like Botticelli's Venus (albeit piously garbed) from a seashell; three extras, one standing, two kneeling, all clad in medieval churchly fashion, and gazing at the Mother of God in mute adoration or well-bred astonishment; two chipped and weatherbeaten *agni Dei*, looking on alertly from the shrubbery; and lovely Olga, seen from the rear, her rich russet hair descending bounteously, her arms clasped over her breasts, her waist small, her hips round and inviting, Olga on the stone bench rocking toward them. After an hour or so Bruno would go down to fetch her, would take her by the hand and lead her home. Then they would make love.

When Olga came home Bruno was stretched out again on the bed. She stood in the doorway embracing two bags stuffed with groceries and glared at him over a head of okra and a bunch of radishes. The climb up the stairs thus laden had winded her slightly. Perspiration sparkled on her upper lip. As late afternoon had given place to early evening the air had grown heavy and humid. Bruno, once more unzipped and still shod, leaned over to switch on the bedside lamp. Olga curled her lip.

"No, don't disturb yourself, gallant gentleman."

Bruno sat up.

"It's not enough the whole neighborhood talks about how we're not married, living across from a church, a blasphemy, how we spit every day on ordinary decency, there's also a school opposite, young children, innocents. Not enough I can't invite my own parents to my home, no, for you this is not enough." Her eyes filled with tears. "In the subway someone tried to stick his thumb up my bottom. I couldn't move, I couldn't even see who. And I have to come from that filth to this, a bum, a no-good, who lies on the bed in shoes." Olga sniffed and turned from him.

Bruno bounded from the bed. "Calm down, let me help you with that."

"Never mind." She was on her way to the kitchen.

Bruno, zipping his pants, lumbered after. "Give me at least one of them."

"Now is a bit late, beau cavalier." She lowered the bags onto the tiny kitchen table. "No, don't touch me. Stand back."

"Olga—"

"Not another word, Bruno. I warn you. I can't take anymore today."

"Olga, for God's sake!"

"Not now." She pushed past him. "I'm going to have a shower. Then we'll eat. Then perhaps we'll talk."

He followed her back into the bedroom. She began to undress. He lay back on the bed, watching her.

She undressed with a compact neatness, not wasting a motion, folding each discarded garment carefully. The moment for the removal of the bra, the last to go, was ordinarily Bruno's favorite. She half-turned towards him. Reaching behind her, she unhooked it, and then in a slight crouch, shoulders forward, she eased it off. The gesture was always followed by a little sigh. The pink nipples stood triumphantly erect. He watched her performance without comment. She shrugged and went into the bathroom.

Bruno lay still. He heard the sound of the shower and soon, rising above it, Olga's voice. She was singing a tune with a Latin rhythm, a series of la-da-dee-dums, followed at measured intervals by a confident *"Viva España!"* The fly on the ceiling walked in a tight circle.

Olga emerged from the bathroom wrapped in a large towel. She stood in the doorway looking at him, all traces of her irritability gone. "A nickel for your thoughts."

Bruno grunted.

"No, for a bum like you a penny is enough." She took short, running steps towards him, the towel constricting her movements. "I'm your little geisha. How can I please you?" Her damp hair fell over his face when she bent over to kiss him. "Pooh, you've had onions."

"Hours ago."

She lay down beside him and ran her fingers over his chest, plucking gently at the hair, kissing his shoulder, his neck, his earlobe. "Do you like me, my samurai?"

Bruno lay still, breathing in her perfume.

She ran her fingers down his body to his unzipped fly, paused, slipped them beneath his underpants and cupped his genitals in her hand. "What have we here? A present for your geisha? Such a little present." Her fingers caressed him, stroked him, grew urgent. She was panting in his ear.

"Ouch!" She had squeezed his testicles too hard. He grabbed her tightly by the wrist, threw her hand from him, released her.

She sprang from the bed, the towel falling from her. The blind fluttered angrily in the window. She turned to face him. Her eyes welled with tears. "You hurt me." Her voice trembled. She put her fists to her eyes like a small child and began to cry.

"I'm sorry. But you hurt *me.*"

"Coward. Coward."

He went to her, held her to him, tried to still her sobbing. She relaxed a little, grew quieter. He bent to kiss her shoulders. "It's all right, I'm sorry, don't cry." She put her arms around him and lifted her face to be kissed. But Bruno, feeling an inexplicable reluctance, stiffened.

Olga put her palms on his chest and pushed him away. "You beast!"

"I've said I'm sorry."

"Yes, yes, you're sorry." She picked up the towel, wiped her eyes with it, held it draped to the floor. She looked at him speculatively. "Today Saul asked me to marry him."

"And?"

"What should I have said?"

"Whatever seemed to you a suitable answer."

"It makes no difference to you?"

"It's your life."

"You swine!" She stamped her heel on the floor. "It's

no use, you have to go, Bruno. It's over. We're through, finished, finito. I can't bear to look at you anymore."

Bruno stared at her for a moment. She stood before him, naked, defiant, her cheeks flushed, her arms akimbo, her foot tapping the floor. He picked up his shirt from the chair where he had carelessly thrown it earlier in the day.

"Not now, you swine! I'm not throwing you into the street. Besides, that's not what happened. Saul's a happily married man." She watched him drop his shirt.

"It was a test?"

"You failed."

"Thanks."

"But very soon, Bruno. I want you out of here. Find your own place. It's over between us. I can't afford you anymore." She clenched her fists. "Today, he fired me. Saul did. I'm out of a job."

"But why?"

"Just because. Who knows why? Because his wife thinks I'm too good-looking for him to have around. Because I'm living in sin. Because I can't work a computer. Who can say? He told me business was bad, the recession. He told me I'm wasting my talents in a dead-end job. 'The world is your oyster,' he said. 'Someday you'll thank me for this.' Then he gave me a check for three months' pay and told me not to come in tomorrow. I've put champagne in the icebox. Later we'll celebrate my freedom." And then she began to sob in earnest.

Bruno went and took her by the hand and led her to the bed. He undressed himself and lay down beside her. He leaned over and kissed her nipples gently, sucked them gently, until her sobbing ceased. She purred deep in her throat. They made love slowly. It had grown dark outside. When the blind flapped, the light from the street lamp entered the room. Only at the end did she suddenly arch her back and tighten her arms and legs around him. She collapsed but would not let him go.

The fly buzzed crazily around the room and landed on the pillow near Olga's head. Bruno flicked it away. She released him and he lay back again.

"An Egyptian fuck," Olga murmured. The phrase, learned from him to describe just such calm and measured lovemaking, a phrase he had dredged from who knew what murky depths of associations, still caused her embarrassment. "Fuck" was a taboo word, an offense against moral tidiness, the language of wicked people. But because this was so, she knew it pleased Bruno to have her say it. And indeed at such moments she was pleased herself. Their lovemaking she thought of as pre-Lenten folly, the license of Mardi Gras, permissible wickedness. She smiled shyly at him, her eyes closed. "An Egyptian fuck?"

"Yes," he said, "an Alexandrian feast."

She lay now in his arms. "I must make dinner." But she was falling asleep. "So good." She nuzzled his chest. "But you must go, Bruno. Soon. I'm not joking. I must find myself a rich man to marry. No more work. . . ." Tiny snores issued from her parted lips.

Bruno could no longer see the fly.

Duncan Greenglass was a fellow of conspicuous charm, florid, with a ready smile, white-toothed, inclined to plumpness and affability. By and large he was quite satisfied with himself. Bruno and Duncan had met at Columbia College, when in their junior year they had worked together on the Follies. Duncan had written the book and lyrics; Bruno, even then a supernumerary, had been cast as a chorus girl. Bruno was the first of his line to attend university, any university. By the time Duncan was born, Columbia was already a Greenglass tradition. He was, you see, one of the Virginia Greenglasses.

It was a familiar story. An itinerant peddler, Lazer Grynglesz, a Polish Jew, who had traveled between and among the contending armies of the American Civil War, pack on back, selling his odds and ends to Blue and Gray alike, careless of bullets, mines and Great Issues, knowing only that all men are brothers, North and South, and that they are endowed by their Creator with certain inalienable needs—tobacco, needles and thread, whiskey, what have you, basic survival gear, needs that he in his humble way might supply—but nevertheless recognizing some time before Appomattox that the Confederate cause was lost and with it the value of Confederate currency, struck down roots in Charlottesville, that is, exchanged his hoard of soon-to-be-worthless Southern dollars for a dry-goods store and a fine white house on a leafy street (purchased from a war widow anxious to flee westward, anywhere away from those vile guns, Jeb bein' daid, and li'l Beauregard scared half out of his wits, y'all gonna like it heah, etc.), buried his Union funds for the duration in a strongbox, found himself a pretty young wife from among the small community of local Israelites, and of Lazer Grynglesz became Laurence Greenglass, Virginian.

Such was the beginning of the Greenglass fortune. Succeeding generations of Greenglasses, while refining out the dross from the rough ore of their great original, honed and sharpened the innate fund of Greenglass business acumen. They branched out, embraced, absorbed, established. Wealth accrued.

Duncan had had no interest whatever in Greenglass Industries, already a public corporation before his birth. Because he would not be idle, the genetic strain still strong, Duncan had bought a foundering weekly newspaper, the *East Side Gazette*, renamed it *Village Culture*, and become both publisher and editor-in-chief. That the enterprise was a success was due in part to his bold editorship and his native business expertise and in part to the high quality of the weekly's news reporting and feature writing. Duncan had worked out an arrangement with Columbia's School of Journalism whereby its most gifted students were offered in exchange for degree credit the chance for on-the-job experience at *Village Culture*. It was an arrangement that pleased everyone and that had earned Duncan a doctorate *honoris causa*.

Today, because the affairs of *Village Culture* had taken

him to the mayor's office, Duncan had made a luncheon reservation at Tavistock's; and because he had wanted a word with his friend Bruno, he had suggested that they meet at the restaurant. He sat at his table, a tumbler of his favorite single-malt whiskey to hand, and worked at a pre-publication copy of his newspaper's English-style crossword puzzle.

Tavistock's was cool, dim and peaceful. To any, however frayed of nerve, who entered through its oaken doors, it offered solace, immediate and absolute. So great a contrast with the outside world often induced a momentary giddiness in the unprepared visitor. Bruno, who had arrived with a minute to spare, stood for a moment catching his breath and adjusting his eyes to the dim light.

From the long bar to his right came the lively hum of muted conversation, discreet laughter, the crisp tinkle of ice cubes against glass. Bruno walked past the line of men and women, movers and shakers, seated and standing, who were refreshing themselves at the gleaming counter, towards the restaurant in the rear.

"There you are," said Duncan genially, not getting up. "Something from the bar?" He signaled the waiter.

"It's a bit early," said Bruno. He sat down.

"Here's one for you," said Duncan, consulting his puzzle. " 'Operatic personage finds herself with ANZAC, after losing feline element of her sharpness.' Seven letters. Anything to do with Melba?"

"Azucena, *Il Trovatore*."

Duncan whistled. "Not bad." He wrote in the name

and checked to see what possibilities that answer had opened up.

"You remember that new production of *Trovatore* at the Buffa three seasons ago? Krauskopf had just come back from London bubbling with a new theory of 'found' dramatic effects?"

"To be honest, no."

"My part was to tend the fire at the Gypsy camp. The curtain hadn't been up five minutes into the second act—this was opening night, mind you—and I'd already created a fiasco."

"We can always rely on you."

"I sauntered out from behind the caravan, golden ear-rings and gold teeth flashing, smacked the bottom of a buxom Gypsy girl, who showed first haughty indignation and then lewd delight—so far so good: still Krauskopf's notion of traditional Romany life. But then I tripped on the wheel and fell into the fire. Consternation throughout the Buffa. The audience gasps. Live coals all over the stage. Thank God they were fake."

"I love it," said Duncan.

"So I pretended it was all part of the act: a stumble-bum Gypsy, comic relief. I picked up the coals—you know, ouch! ouch!—as if they were burning my fingers, got the fire together again in a heap under the steaming kettle. But there was this one lump that had rolled under Azucena's skirt. I mean, Azucena knew nothing: I could scarcely lift Elvira Königsberger's skirt. So Elvira's busy singing 'Stride la vampa'—you know, how di Luna's father had burned

her mother as a witch, her fear of the flames, and so on——
and all the while smoke's curling up from under her skirt.
For all they knew in the audience, her holy of holies might
have been on fire."

"Elvira has a reputation," said Duncan.

"Meanwhile, Guido Krauskopf is ecstatic. This is what
he meant, he tells us afterwards, this is what they're doing
in London: the 'found' dramatic effect. It's deep, he says.
Meaningful. Keep it, he says. It's a concrete metaphor."

"Guido's no fool," said Duncan.

The waiter minced over with his pad. "Nice day, Mr.
Greenglass."

"It's a scorcher, Tim, it's lousy. You're lucky you're
inside. Anything to recommend?"

"They're pushing the scrod," said Tim, "which is nice
and fresh, but you take my advice you'll go for the poached
salmon. It's stuffed with crabmeat."

"The salmon it is, then. Bruno?"

"The same."

"Is Jimmy in today? . . . Good. Have him prepare a
salad, my usual."

Tim removed himself, swiftly and discreetly.

"Not that I object, Duncan, but to what do I owe
today's lunch?"

In a dim corner of Tavistock's, Elvira Königsberger sat
in close conclave with Guido Krauskopf. She looked up and
saw Bruno, half-waved, and whispered in Krauskopf's ear.

Duncan nodded his head towards the corner and glanced
at Bruno shrewdly. "You been in to see Guido yet? It's not

my business, but he's sitting on something new, something he wants to offer you. Could be the making of you."

"Okay, I'll bite. What's he got?"

Duncan raised a forefinger to his lips. "That's not for me to say. Trust me, it's worth your while to go see him. Soon."

Together they looked again into the corner. Elvira and Krauskopf were head to head. Elvira laughed suddenly; Krauskopf took her beringed fingers and kissed her gallantly on the knuckles. Elvira simpered; Krauskopf picked up his glass and toasted her. It was a performance. They were in Tavistock's not so much to see as to be seen.

"It's a bit awkward, Bruno. Not quite sure how to put it." Duncan swirled the ice in his glass. "Olga came to see me a few days ago. Looking for a job, she said. Perhaps I had a vacancy, perhaps I knew of someone who had."

"Saul Lustig fired her."

"So she said."

Tim arrived with salmon and salad. Bruno and Duncan began to eat.

"You don't have to give her a job for my sake."

"That's not it." Duncan actually blushed. "The thing is, I don't think she was really looking for a job. She knew whatever she told me would get back to you. So okay, I already knew the two of you haven't been hitting it off too well of late. For that, Olga scarcely needed to come by. I mean, you don't have to be a clairvoyant."

"It's over, Duncan. At first, she told me she wanted me to move out, which was fine with me. But in fact, she moved out herself. A week ago. I got home to find her gone. She hadn't taken much. Oh, and she left a note: 'Go or stay, Bruno. I don't care what you do. I'm out of here.' No forwarding address."

Duncan looked shyly at Bruno, still testing the waters. "She's found herself a gentleman companion, a rich Russian."

So that was it! Bruno, to his surprise, felt a sharp pang of jealousy, a sour sense of betrayal. But why? He had long wished to be rid of her. He should rejoice. The truth is, he missed her, missed the bickering, missed her body beside him on the bed, missed a thousand unidentifiable impressions and sensations of daily living. In a letter to his father, Mozart had complained of his misery when circumstances had temporarily separated him from his Constanze. She was not good-looking, she was not even a good housekeeper; but without her, Mozart felt he was living a "half-life." And why should Bruno be smarter than Mozart?

"Good for her," he said.

Duncan seemed relieved. "You don't mind, then?"

"Perhaps he'll marry her. It's what she's always wanted. The ideal solution, for her, for me." He looked around for the waiter. "I'd like that drink now, okay? Let's drink to their happiness, to my freedom."

Duncan signaled to the attentive Tim.

"She's a grownup, she can do what she likes."

"Relationships," sighed Duncan. "They can be a bitch."

"You should know."

It was true that when Duncan fell in love he fell completely; it was also true that he fell rather too frequently. His heart he gave again and again. The frail bark of his fourth marriage, the most recent, splintered beyond salvage when Pauline burst unannounced (and of course unexpected) into his private office on West Eighth Street and found him introducing himself into his secretary, his affirmative action employee, a young black woman of quite apparent beauty. It was an unfortunate irony that Pauline herself had chosen the tufted leather couch as a complement to Duncan's office decor.

In the corner Elvira Königsberger and Guido Krauskopf made a great show of getting up. They swept towards the exit, Elvira hanging passionately on to Krauskopf's arm, the two of them chatting animatedly. Elvira turned suddenly towards Bruno, flashed him a brilliant smile, and blew him a kiss. Bruno made as if to catch it and convey it to his lips, and then, gallantly, he blew one back. Elvira laughed in toothy delight. She and Krauskopf resumed their passage, waving regally at this table or that as they went by.

"You and Elvira—you're not, so to speak, a number, are you?"

"Give me a break, Duncan. She could be my mother."

"Oedipus shmoedipus. She's still a hot number, is Elvira."

"Very funny."

"Go and see Guido," said Duncan earnestly. "Do yourself a favor."

Guarding the open stage-door entrance to the Buffa was Lev Krauskopf, pudgy, ugly, adolescent son of the manager and director. He sat hunched over on a high stool against the crumbling brick wall, his eyes closed, earphones on his head, a Walkman in his breast pocket, swaying and snapping his fingers.

Bruno poked him in the stomach. "Your dad in, Lev?"

Lev opened his eyes, saw Bruno, closed his eyes again, and increased the enthusiasm of his swaying and finger-snapping, as if an audience, however small, required of him his visible rhythmic best.

"Is he in his office?"

Lev swayed and snapped his fingers.

Bruno pushed the earphones back over Lev's head, until they fell into an embrace of his neck.

Lev opened his eyes, which registered emotional pain. "Hey!" he said. "Hey, you didn't have t'do that. Y'know? You didn't have t'do that, hey."

"Your dad?"

"I'm only here till Jimmy gets back. He's taking a leak out back. Musta needed to go real bad, I been here for twenty minutes, maybe more. Yeah, Dad's down in props. Wanna guess who's with him?" Lev snickered. "Watch out, Cindy!"

Bruno walked past him into the dank interior and made for the basement stairs.

"I'm listening to the Dedd Hedds," Lev called after him. "Their new album. So you'll understand I can't just sit here and talk."

The basement smelled of wet concrete, rotting wood and curry. Bruno knocked on a fire door marked "Props. Keep Out. Authorized Personnel Only."

"Fuck off!" came a voice, strangulated but recognizably belonging to Guido Krauskopf.

"It's Bruno."

A pause; then: "Bruno? Great! Hey, give me a minute, okay?" Muted, indecipherable sounds. "C'mon in, Bruno."

The props room was lighted by a single bulb of low wattage that hung naked from the ceiling. Banks of props disappeared into a surrounding gloom. Highly visible, however, was Guido Krauskopf, who sat on the gilded throne of *Aida*, the cap and bells of *Rigoletto* on his head, the fool's belled bauble in his hand. His forehead was beaded with sweat.

"You know my secretary, Cindy?" he said, pointing with his tinkling bauble towards a packing case half-hidden in the gloom, on which sat a young woman, her blond hair in disarray, her lipstick smeared, and her blouse misbuttoned. "Cindy, this is Bruno Sorge."

"Please t'meetch'all," said Cindy, winking and smoothing her skirt over her spread thighs.

"Cindy," said Krauskopf, "Bruno and me, we've got business to discuss. You'll understand, we need a bit of privacy, okay?"

Cindy looked a trifle perplexed.

"Cindy," said Krauskopf sweetly. "Get the fuck outta here."

Cindy got to her feet and made for the door. "See ya, Bruno."

Krauskopf, with his bauble, beckoned Bruno forward, indicating the recently vacated packing case. "Sit down, for God's sake. Make yourself comfortable." He eyed Bruno speculatively. "Listen, we're both men of the world. This means nothing. Why upset Cherie, right?"

"I saw Lev outside. A fine boy."

"You bet. Takes after Cherie, bless her. But adolescence is a painful period, painful. Remember how it was? The zits? Just the same, I see a glimmering of intellectual acuity in that boy. Could be there's my replacement. Lev might be it." He pointed his bauble at Bruno. "So how's Olga, how's my favorite Roumanian?"

"Hungarian."

"Same difference. That's some girl you've got yourself there." He sighed. "You're a lucky guy, Bruno."

Bruno bit his lip. "You said you wanted to see me?"

"You ready for the big time, Bruno? You ready?" He waved his bauble sternly at Bruno. "Let me put you in the picture. We call ourselves the Buffa, right? Never mind we also do heavy stuff, not just buffa: *Butterfly*, *Don Giovanni*, *Traviata*. The classics, right? Okay, nothing wrong with that. But something's missing. What is it?" He waved his bauble in the configuration of a question mark. "I'll tell you what's missing. The American musical, that's what's missing. *Oklahoma!*, *West Side Story*, *My Fair Lady*."

"*Chu Chin Chow*," offered Bruno.

"I'm not kidding around," said Krauskopf, aggrieved. "The American musical is the culmination of a long history: commedia dell'arte, buffa, opera, grand opera, operetta—finally, the American musical. You think Bernstein is peanuts? You think Sondheim is just jerking off? I know, I know. You'll tell me, so what? You'll tell me, even if we get permission, no guarantee, the royalties alone will wipe us out. You're right, I'll admit it. When you're right, you're right." He leaned back on his throne, smirking as if he'd just won an argument.

"Fascinating," said Bruno dryly. "But what has any of this to do with me?"

Krauskopf ignored the interruption. "The answer is to go for something new, something the world knows nothing about. I've come into a property—such a property!—could be *Fiddler on the Roof* for our time. Bruno, I'm going to make you a star. Never mind *I* wanted you for the part, Elvira insisted on it. We'll open down here, but we're heading for Broadway. Hold tight!"

"You should know, your fly's unzipped, your shirt's hanging out."

Krauskopf looked down. "I'm talking art here, not high fashion. Besides, I need to take a leak. 'A business must always stay open.' " He reached for a brown-paper package on the trunk beside his throne and stood. "Here it is, book and lyrics," he said reverently. "Better than *Fiddler*."

"I can't sing," said Bruno, getting up. "You know that."

"That's the beauty part. The male lead's all patter. Remember Rex Harrison? You think he was a singer? Elvira will coach you." He handed Bruno the package. "Take it home, study it. Phone me tomorrow, tell me what you think. You'll be down on your knees thanking me."

"Who's doing the music?"

Krauskopf put his arm around Bruno's shoulders and led him towards the door. "A natural enough question, but not your concern. Let's just say we're working on it."

"What about my salary?"

"Read it," said Krauskopf. "Just read it. Time enough to talk about money."

☙

Although the lace counterpane was one of the few personal items, apart from her clothes, that Olga had packed and taken away with her, Bruno carefully removed his shoes before making himself comfortable, fully clothed, upon the bed and opening the package that Krauskopf had given him. He turned to the title page, and what he saw there caused his mouth to drop open. No wonder Duncan had urged him to see Krauskopf!

Dreyfus: The Musical

Book and Lyrics
by
Duncan Greenglass

Was Duncan having him on? Was this an elaborate hoax, one involving not only Krauskopf but necessarily Elvira as well? Yet, if it was a hoax, they would all have to be in on it. A musical about *Dreyfus*? It *must* be a joke, it *had* to be. On the other hand, it was also inconceivable that they should employ so much energy merely to make a fool of him, of Bruno.

He read through the manuscript with mounting dismay. It was a tissue of clichés, clichés of character, of language, of situation, of setting, of story line. Its lyrics were feeble parodies of songs, not even disguised, songs universally familiar. It took a serious subject and made a fatuous mockery of it. It was deeply offensive. And Duncan had written *this*? He flipped through the pages, pausing first at Act I, scene 2:

> *A brothel in Paris frequented by French officers. At a table bearing champagne bottles and glasses sit two lieutenants, uniforms in disarray, playing cards, their laps occupied by* filles de joie. ESTERHAZY *is perhaps twenty-two, gaunt and unhealthy-looking;* D'ALEMBERT *is much older, in his mid-forties, plump, with fully developed English muttonchop whiskers, a red face, and an air of drunken good humor. The* filles de joie *are not in their first youth. The fat one sits on the thin lieutenant's lap and* vice versa. *Stage left, rear, a man behind the bar is wiping glasses. A third lieutenant,* VALOMBRE, *a booby, an overgrown boy, his hair and his moustaches crisped without doubt by hot irons, leans against the bar and waves his glass blearily in time to the music tinkled by a piano player*

at stage right. The proprietress, MADAME JUPPÉ, *feathers rising from her coiffed hair, a boa around her neck, strokes the bald spot at the back of the piano player's head.*

As the lights in the brothel grow dim and finally go out, a small area aloft is increasingly illuminated. It is revealed as a cluttered dressing room. Stairs lead from it to the darkened stage below. In the dressing room we see a YOUNG WOMAN *in a chorus girl's spangled costume and black net stockings. She is remarkably like the Marlene Dietrich of* The Blue Angel. *She is finishing her toilette, primping before the mirror, adjusting her hair, straightening the seam on her stockings, trying and rejecting various bangles and beads, etc. She begins to sing. Her voice is sensuous and deep; her accent is would-be French.*

Schmetterling Song

SCHMETTERLING:

They call me Schmetterling, a butterfly.
Oh, do not castigate me,
Do not formulate me,
Do not pin me to the wall.
Ach, no. Ach, no. Ach, no,
Ach, do not pin me to the wall.
They say I'm Schmetterling, the Hunnish spy.
Ach, do not analyze me,
Do not supervise me,
You cannot plumb my depths at all.
Ach, no. Ach, no. Ach, no,
You cannot plumb my depths at all.
     For . . . I . . . was born . . . for love;
     It is my gift,

Culled from Above.
Since . . . I . . . can give . . . you joy,
No more be miffed,
You lucky boy!
For I am Schmetterling, now you know why.
With me there is no sorrow,
There is no tomorrow,
Love me today; forget you'll die.

(She removes a spangled top hat from a hook on the wall, plonks it triumphantly and rakishly on her curls, takes a last look at herself, and comes to the top of the stairs, where she pauses and where, while the lights of the dressing room dim and go out behind her, she is picked up by a spotlight. The music continues, and the lower stage is reilluminated, to reveal the officers, who, as the music swells, become reanimated.)

ESTERHAZY:

Look, gentlemen, Mademoiselle Schmetterling!

D'ALEMBERT:

Mademoiselle! At last!

VALOMBRE:

Alphonse! *(He is addressing the man at the bar.)* Champagne! Lots of it!

(The officers rush to the foot of the stairs, where they arrange themselves in gestures of ardor. MADAME JUPPÉ, but more sedately, joins them. LOU-LOU and FROU-FROU, the two filles de joie, *looking bedraggled, sit themselves at the table and disconsolately pick*

*up the cards. Schmetterling begins her descent, sinu-
ously, sexily, slowly, beaming at the OFFICERS, who
meanwhile sing to her the Schmetterling Song, suitably
altered.)*

Schmetterling Song (Reprise)

ESTERHAZY, D'ALEMBERT, VALOMBRE:
They call her Schmetterling, a butterfly.
Oh, do not castigate her,
Do not formulate her *(etc.)* . . .

*(As they finish the song, she reaches the foot of the
stairs. Teasingly, laughingly, she gives each of them a
kiss but manages to evade their embraces.)*

The script was scarcely improved by a second reading.
Crap, crap, nothing but crap. Bruno flipped forward to
Act III, scene 1.

*Outside the barracks: a wall of hewn stone, in which
is set the heavy gate. No guard is in sight. Time:
midnight. The only illumination is provided by a lantern affixed high to the wall. We hear the sudden
barking of a dog, then an angry cry to silence it. Enter,
slowly, stage right, two figures, SCHMETTERLING and
LIEUTENANT DREYFUS. They are obviously in love.
They pause, a little to the left of the gate and beneath
the lantern.*

SCHMETTERLING:
You must go then, beloved?

DREYFUS:

I must, my little cabbage. It is my duty.

SCHMETTERLING:

If only . . .

DREYFUS:

If only . . .

(Music. He takes both her hands in his and raises them to his lips. She gazes at him in adoration, then takes the rose from behind her ear and twists its stem around a button on his tunic.)

SCHMETTERLING:

Wear it for me.

DREYFUS:

Forever.

SCHMETTERLING:

But perhaps one day when nations live in peace with one another, when there are no narrow distinctions separating a man from the woman he loves, perhaps in that world made new again . . .

DREYFUS:

There are no buts, my little butterfly.

SCHMETTERLING:

I know.

The Affair

(They are picked up, discreetly, unobtrusively, by a spotlight. Still holding hands, they sing their Love Duet.)

Love Duet

SCHMETTERLING:
If you were the only Jew in the world,

DREYFUS:
And you were the only goy.

SCHMETTERLING, DREYFUS:
No adverse conditions would stand in our way,
We would test the limits of erotic play.

SCHMETTERLING:
A vessel of pleasure: we'd be the crew.

DREYFUS:
I tremble to think . . . Hoo boy!

SCHMETTERLING, DREYFUS:
First we'd snuggle up and then we'd kitchy-koo,
Then before we knew it we'd begin to screw.

SCHMETTERLING:
If you were the only Jew in the world,

DREYFUS:
And you were the only goy.

*(The music continues the melody, to which Mlle.
SCHMETTERLING and Lieutenant DREYFUS dance a
stately, poignant waltz, brought to an end when they
sing a reprise of their Love Duet's refrain. The violins
are prominent here, hopeless, bittersweet. After all, in
the wings, History beckons.)*

SCHMETTERLING:
If you were the only Jew in the world,

DREYFUS:
And you were the only goy.

*(Mlle. SCHMETTERLING removes a handkerchief from
her bosom, blows her nose, and, racked with sobs,
makes for the stage right wing. The music is strong
here, perhaps using a Doom Theme, such as that from
La Forza del Destino. When she has disappeared
from view, Lieutenant DREYFUS squares his shoulders
and marches courageously through the gate. Curtain.)*

Bruno tossed the script onto the coffee table and got
up. He paced the room, back and forth. Duncan had taken
his years of work, his patient if sporadic research, his most
sacred intent, and trampled on them. The treachery sick-
ened him. He picked up the script again, flipping the pages:
Act I, scene 3.

*Lieutenant Dreyfus's spartan quarters: a metal cot, be-
side which is a small cabinet, a wash basin, and a
pitcher; a narrow armoire; on the whitewashed wall a
photograph of Schmetterling; an open window; just left
of stage center, a table piled high with military tomes,*

some open. Lieutenant DREYFUS *is burning the midnight oil. He is seated with military erectness behind the table and scribbling in a notebook. Briefly, a sound of drunken revelry is heard from without, then it is again silent. The lieutenant stops writing. He takes off his steel-rimmed glasses and rubs the bridge of his nose.*

DREYFUS:

Ach, why do I bother with all this? What hope is there? As an officer I'm regarded as a joke. My superiors scarcely trouble to mask their disdain; my juniors pretend not to notice me. Better to have joined the ranks. Perhaps someone then might have noticed the field marshal's baton in my knapsack. *(He gets up and comes towards the footlights. He is picked up by a spotlight.)* And what's their reason? None of them will say it, but it doesn't take a genius to know. All my life I've wanted to be a soldier, an officer, to lead the charge, to serve France. And I've come so close! It doesn't bear thinking about. *(Music begins.)* My dream of glory remains a dream, increasingly improbable.

Song: The Improbable Dream

DREYFUS:

If you're eager to do fine
In a military line
As a soldier brave and true,
You will find the going tough,
You will find your messmates rough,
If you also are a Jew.

Though von Clausewitz you've studied,
Though you dream of being bloodied,
It will all boil down to this:
You lack soci-al mobility,
Are cut off from nobility,
Just because you've had a *bris*.
For the Gen'ral Staff will sneer
With hostility and fear,
"If a foreskin's not for him, what it certainly is
    for me,
Why, what a singularly vile young man this
    vile young man must be."

Though I pay the honor owed
To the Military Code
And have gotten it by heart,
My comrades merely mock,
For they're thinking of my cock,
And not my martial art.
Just a *miles gloriosus*
With a comical proboscis—
That's what my colonel sees.
Let him hear my saber rattle
As I lead men into battle:
There's the foe upon his knees!
Then the Gen'ral Staff will shout,
As I carve a bloody rout,
"If a foreskin's not for him, it's most certainly
    not for me.
My, what a singularly brave young man, a
    brave young Jew must be!"

Bruno threw the manuscript across the room. He was
stung by the enormity of the betrayal. He had shown Dun-

can his essay and his plans for a book in good faith, hoping for an assessment, for guidance. He got up and went to the phone.

"Tell me you're kidding."

"Okay, I'm kidding."

"Thank God!"

"Bruno, what are we talking about?"

"*Dreyfus*. We're talking about *Dreyfus: The Musical*. What did you *think* we were talking about?"

"You've read it?" said Duncan eagerly. "Well? What d'you think of it?"

"More laughs than a barrel of monkeys. Duncan, you *can't* write a musical about Dreyfus, it's obscene."

" 'Obscene'? Well, I suppose some of the raunchier passages could be toned down a bit. But nowadays, with full frontal nudity and the f-word de rigueur behind the footlights, gee, I don't know. Some might think it a bit tame."

"That's not what I meant by 'obscene.' Dreyfus is a serious subject."

"So? *West Side Story* wasn't serious? *Evita* wasn't serious? Think about it. My court-martial scene? Isn't that serious? Dreyfus's solo on Devil's Island: that's not serious?"

"A hundred years on and Dreyfus is still splitting France. He's a Jewish *martyr*, for pity's sake. You trivialize him, make a mockery of him. You'll offend the entire Jewish community, worldwide."

"They'll love it. Trust me."

"And those lyrics, they're nothing but parodies."

" 'Pastiche' is the word you want. Besides, the allusions become more subtle when they're set to new tunes."

"You've got a composer?"

"Of *course* I've got a composer. Lauritz Mossbacher, Guido's brother-in-law."

"You're putting your own money into this madness?"

"Enough to grease the wheels."

"Don't you give a shit about me?"

"Of course I do. You're my buddy. This is your big break. Didn't Guido tell you?"

"You've stolen my work, my ideas."

"Hold on a minute, simmer down. You've got no copyright on history. Sure, I read your essay. So what? There are hundreds of books on Dreyfus, maybe thousands. You want to see my bibliography? Besides, the musical can only help you. Dreyfus'll become hot again. I'll put out the word. Publishers will be beating at your door." But something of his friend's tone had at last penetrated the stronghold of Duncan's certainty. "Stop kidding around, for God's sake. Tell me what you really think."

"It's crap, Duncan. It's total crap. You wrote better stuff for the Follies." Silence. "Duncan?"

"With an attitude like that," said Duncan coldly, "I don't see how you can expect to play Dreyfus."

"I have no intention of playing Dreyfus. Can't you understand what I'm saying? No one should play Dreyfus, no one *will* play Dreyfus, not *this* Dreyfus. You've had your fun, the creative juices have flowed, it's time to quit."

"Thank you, Bruno Sorge, for your inestimable advice. Now here's a bit of advice from me: drop dead." And Duncan slammed down the receiver.

Zvi Elsasser was a neat, compact man of perhaps seventy with close-cropped hair and a pale face. He affected subdued business suits, white-on-white shirts, and rich, somber ties. At his cuffs, links of heavy gold gleamed; his fingernails sparkled with clear varnish. Otherwise, he presented what might be called a matte finish. In fact, he looked somewhat like a successful accountant from Queens—which he had been until about twenty years ago, when he had bought a dying opera company in the Village, the d'Avanzo, and turned it around, for a while his ledgers actually showing a profit. Now, as everyone knew, times were tough.

With admirable economy Elsasser paused in the act of conveying soup to his mouth and with the arrested spoon gestured to Bruno to sit down opposite him. He spilled not a drop. "Sorry to have dragged you all the way out here." "Here" was a new bistro and nightclub called Raskolnikov's that stood beneath the rusting blight of the el on Brighton Beach Avenue in Brooklyn. "Here" was where Elsasser had told Bruno he could fit him into his crowded schedule—"I can give you maybe forty-five minutes, fifty at most"—when Bruno had phoned him to suggest they talk about next season.

Elsasser handed him a menu. "First we must get you

something to eat. Pick whatever you like, it's all good, don't hold back. My advice, you'll go for the borscht, what I've got here, Ukrainian, goes down a treat. Waiter!"

Raskolnikov's bright interior was all marble and gilt and plum-colored velvet swaggery. At the far end of the room stood a small semicircular stage with a mirrored edging, on which sat a plump young woman in a kind of diaphanous toga draped over a sequined bikini. She smiled vacuously and strummed, inaudible above the restaurant's chatter, a balalaika. A bottle of vodka stood on every table, the refreshment of choice. And nearly every table was taken; the rising hubbub, fueled perhaps by the plentiful vodka, was in Russian. It was, in fact, in Russian that Elsasser spoke to the waiter.

"Bet you didn't know I could do that, huh, Bruno? Talk in Russian?" Elsasser beamed. "Came over in 1935, a *pishika,* ten years old, didn't know a word of English. Sixty years later, for sixty years only English, not a syllable of Russian, and look at me: I didn't forget a thing."

"Remarkable," said Bruno flatly. "But I know you're a busy man. So, shall we talk?"

"You think I've forgotten my manners, I'm a boor, a *greener*? When you're eating your soup we'll talk. Meanwhile, I've ordered some more of this bread, wait till you taste it." Elsasser tore off a small chunk and neatly wiped the bottom of his soup bowl with it. "What do you think of this place? Pretty fancy, huh? Better than the Winter Palace, people say." He leaned forward and lowered his voice to a whisper, forcing Bruno to lean towards him.

"It's a big favorite with the Russian *mafiya*. They eat at only the best places. Look over there, for example—not *now*, shmuck, in a minute, I'll tell you when—over there, under the portrait of Pushkin, sitting with the good-looker in sunglasses, that's Yuri Voloshin, one of the biggest, worth millions, don't ask. He's what they call a *vory v zakone*—in English you'd say a 'thief-in-law,' what the Sicilians call a 'made man.' "

The waiter gave Bruno his soup and placed a basket of crusty brown bread on the table.

"Okay, now you can look," whispered Elsasser. "Only, make it casual."

Bruno turned and saw a sandy-haired, bearded brute of a fellow, with tufts of hair rioting from the open neck of an electric-blue silk shirt. Dead, piggy eyes, sunk in an overblown pink face, glared at the glass of vodka in his hand. Around his neck hung a large black cross, studded with gems. His table companion, "the good-looker in sunglasses" sitting next to him, a smaller albeit otherwise identical cross resting on her bosom, was Olga, heavily made up. Bruno quickly turned away.

"Eat, Bruno, eat. Don't let it get cold."

Bruno, shocked into obedience, swallowed a mouthful of soup. So this was Olga's Russian, this her protector. Inwardly, he recoiled. He did not know whether what he felt was jealousy or anger. That she should have shifted herself so smoothly from him, from Bruno Sorge, to this . . . this . . . this porcine thug! It passed belief. He turned again, briefly, towards her, to confirm that it was indeed she and caught Voloshin in mid-belch. Dimly, he became aware that Elsasser was talking to him.

". . . know when it's time to move on, no point in beating a dead horse, the Village, trust me, is finished . . ."

Was it sex? Yes, that must be it. This animal Voloshin, unhampered by civilization's restraints, had, no doubt, lifted her to heights of ecstasy impossible to the guiding principles of a man of humane sensibility. Oh, Olga, Olga! To what unimaginable sex games has he swinishly led you?

". . . and that's it in a nutshell."

"Sorry, Zvi. My mind was elsewhere." But Bruno sensed Olga passing behind him. He turned with deliberate slowness and saw her retreating figure disappear around a corner, making for what must be the ladies' room. He got up. "Excuse me a moment, I've got to go to the john."

"Shall I have them keep your soup warm?"

"The soup's fine. I'll be back in a moment."

He turned the corner. Yes, there was the ladies' room. Opposite was the men's. He went in but kept the door slightly ajar, his eye on the ladies'. When she reappeared, he emerged.

"Hey, Olga! What a surprise! How's it going?"

"Fine. How about you?"

"Fine, fine. You're looking good. You happy?"

"Happy? You bet."

He nodded at the cross between her breasts. "You've found religion, I see."

"I never lost it. It was you, Bruno. It was you made me spit on my religion."

"Sure, sure. Tell me, what's with the sunglasses? You're indoors."

"The lights. It's so bright in here, they bother my eyes."

But Bruno saw an area of discoloration high on her left cheek, where it emerged beneath the sunglasses. "He's beating you up. He gave you a black eye."

"You're crazy. I fell. I hurt myself."

"So how's the sex? Must be great, must be like being fucked by a horse, a donkey at least."

"You're disgusting, Bruno," she said bitterly. "You'll never change. Never. Yuri wants to marry me. I'm going to be his wife. He treats a woman with respect."

"Come home, Olga. Please." He put a restraining hand on her forearm, but she tore it free.

"I've got to go."

"You've *got* to go?"

"I *want* to go." She turned from him and made for the dining room.

He waited a moment and then followed her in, seating himself again opposite Elsasser.

"Your soup's cold."

"It doesn't matter. I'm not hungry."

"So what do you say?"

"I'm sorry, Zvi. You're going to have to go through it again."

"Jesus Christ!" Elsasser looked angrily and pointedly at his watch. "All right, I can give you six more minutes, a quick rundown. Do me a favor, pay attention, you should be so kind. The Village is Gonzo City. I'm moving the whole operation here. We're working with the community and with the mayor's office. It's serious. We're underwritten. They're fixing up the old Roxy on Continental Avenue exclusively for our use. The place is crawling with Russians, new immigrants. You'd be surprised at the talent. We've got kids here, graduates of the Moscow Conservatory. Not only that, we've got a built-in audience. They're starving for culture out here. It's like the Lower East Side when I came to America. Only, we've got to shift to Russian opera. That's what they want. Okay, no problem. We're opening with Rimsky-Korsakov's *The Tsar's Bride*. You know it? Okay, never mind.

"So where do you come in? Frankly, I don't know. Supernumeraries we can use, but where someone of your special talents fits in"—here Elsasser essayed a sneer—"I haven't figured out yet. Russian opera requires singers. On the other hand, Elvira insists that we hire you or we can forget about her. On the third hand, I'm not so sure about Elvira. What does *she* know about Russian opera? *Bubkes*. Besides, she's got something going with Krauskopf. What, I don't know. The truth is, I don't care. I'm moving out here with or without her. Here is where it's at.

"So we come back to you, Bruno. I can offer you for sure only supernumerary parts, but, because that's the kind of guy I am, at the salary I gave you for Selim Pasha, guaranteed. I'm ruining myself, but I've known you for a long time. What do you say?"

Bruno turned to look at Olga. Voloshin was talking with

bloated animation to their waiter, the thumb of one hand indicating Olga's breasts. Suddenly, he seized her left breast, cupping it in his other hand; he moved it up and down as if he were weighing it. He and the waiter laughed. Olga, in her shame, looked aside, saw the fleshy balalaika player nodding to her knowingly, and closed her eyes.

"That's me as Zerlina," said Elvira. "Milano. Mario Conti was Don Giovanni, Enrico Tozzi conducting."

They stood before the full-length portrait of the young Elvira hung above the fireplace in her living room. She had invited Bruno to her apartment. They had things to talk about. He should come as he was. Nothing fancy, just the two of them. Champagne, caviar, why not? And later? Who knew?

"La Scala?" said Bruno.

Elvira ignored the question. "It was painted by Boris Kaunas. Of course, you know his work? Naturally. It's unmistakable. There were rumors about the two of us, naughty stories." She laughed gaily, almost spilling her champagne. "Not all of them true."

For yes, there was champagne, although no caviar. Elvira had broached the first bottle before his arrival and was already well along by the time she flung the door open to greet him. "Come in, come in, sweetie!" She waved him in, sloshing the champagne in her glass, mouthing a kiss as he passed her, pinching him on the cheek. "Alone at last."

Elvira was clad in a fuchsia negligée, ruffled at top and bottom. Her face was a mask of makeup, her rubbery lips a vivid carmine, her eyelids a silvered blue and edged with long curling lashes. She wore her bright red hair *en bouffant*.

In the living room she poured champagne for him and topped up her own glass, spilling some over the rim with bleary abandon. "Whoops!" She sat herself opposite him, crossing her still-shapely legs and drawing the skirts of her negligée over her knees with the kind of seductive modesty that drew attention to them. Her glass held waveringly before her, she offered a toast. "To us, to me and my handsome co-star! To *Dreyfus: The Musical!*" She tilted back her head and chug-a-lugged.

"Not me, Elvira. I've already spoken to Duncan."

"I know, I know. He told me. But you're going to change your mind. *I'm* going to change it for you." She refilled her glass. "Come along, sweetie, drink up. There's lots more in the icebox." She shook her head and smiled at him, as a fond parent might whose clever child has committed an easily correctible error. "Ah, Bruno, Bruno, what am I going to do with you? You *are* Dreyfus. It's the role you were born to play. No, don't interrupt. I'm going to convince you. Before you leave here—perhaps, we'll see, after breakfast, who knows?—you're going to phone Duncan and give him the good news. But first let me tell you a little story."

The little story she told was the story of her life. She was born Elsie King, "never mind when," in Brooklyn, a stone's throw from the Brooklyn Academy of Music. " 'BAM,' we called it. 'Bim-bam, thank you ma'am.' " She giggled and fluttered her lashes girlishly. "Naughty me!" "Königsberger" had been her father's name in the old country; he changed it in his eagerness to become a genuine American. "Ironic, when you think of it. When I started out, you couldn't get anywhere in opera, not here in America, with a name like Elsie King." She paused, in need of refreshment, drank dreamily, peering into her past, and then resumed her tale. She told of her early promise, her years of study, the beginning of her career. The story turned bleak. She had had no luck; she had been too often in the wrong place at the wrong time. Too easily, far too easily, she had given away her heart and the direction of her life to a series of second-raters, agents, tenors, producers, managers—"no-goodniks, bums, cheats." They had sworn they loved her, had her career foremost in their minds, but they had sold her down the river for short-term gains. Always she had reached for the brass ring; always it had eluded her grasp. "I should be singing today at the Met, at Covent Garden, in Vienna. So where am I singing? In Greenwich Village."

Her tale finished, she took Bruno by the hand and led him on a tour of the many photographs, certificates and citations that decorated her living-room walls, an illustrated biography that culminated with the Kaunas portrait, Elvira as Zerlina, the high point of her career and its beginning. "This time, I'll get the brass ring, this time it's mine!" Impulsively, she flung her arms around his neck and drew him to her, cushioning him in her generous bosom. He felt a cold liquid on his neck, felt it trickling down his spine. "And I'm taking you with me, Bruno, right to the top." Elvira plastered her open mouth on his, and forced her tongue between his teeth. He was granted a taste of champagne so powerfully concentrated as to make him reel. Then she released him, lifted the bottle from the ice bucket, and emptied the remains into her glass. "*Dreyfus* is what I've been waiting for all my life."

Bruno recovered from her assault. "Come off it, Elvira. You must *know* that *Dreyfus* is pure crap."

"You're wrong—you've only seen the book. You'd say the same about *The Magic Flute* if you'd only read the book. Listen to this. Do me a favor, just listen to this." And Elvira tottered over to the piano, placed her champagne glass with elaborate care upon it, and sat before the keyboard. She glanced at him before tossing off an arpeggio and then, accompanying herself, began to sing:

> "They call me Schmetterling, a butterfly.
> Oh, do not castigate me,
> Do not formulate me,
> Do not pin me to the wall."

She looked at him.

Well, yes, thought Bruno, it has something.

"Now listen to this." Elvira played again. "Did you hear it? The ascending seventh in the last bar?" She played it again. "Pure crap? Give me a break. Pure genius!"

The truth is, she almost had Bruno convinced. "Okay, let's say, for the sake of argument, it's 'pure genius.' What's in it for you?"

Elvira got up from the piano, turned, and stood swaying before him. She retrieved her glass and narrowed her eyes. "What d'you mean, what's in it for me?"

"Well, what role do you see for yourself? Surely, there's not much in *Dreyfus* for you. Madame Juppé, the brothel keeper? But she doesn't even have an aria—a song, I should say—of her own. Dreyfus's mother? Sarah Bernhardt? But she makes only a cameo appearance. What's it got that interests you?"

"What are you talking about, stupid? Madame Juppé? Sarah Bernhardt? What've they to do with me? I'm Schmetterling, shmuck. I'm the female lead."

Bruno emitted a spontaneous laugh. "But Schmetterling's a girl, twenty at most. How could you play . . . ?" Even as he spoke, he read with horror the folly of his words on Elvira's face. "I mean . . ."

"Get out," said Elvira icily. She took her glass to her lips, tilted back her head, and swallowed. Her fury mounted. "Get out, you fucking creep!" she screamed.

"But Elvira—"

"Get out!"

Bruno turned to go. He heard her sobbing behind him. She hurled her glass at his retreating back, hitting him with accuracy between his shoulder blades, the glass falling thence to the floor, miraculously unbroken.

"You'll never work in this town again!"

Time passed, six months, a year, eighteen months. Meanwhile, *Dreyfus: The Musical* had become a *succès fou*. After six smash-hit weeks at the Buffa, it had moved to Broadway, the newly refurbished David Richter Theater, where it played to SRO crowds. There was not a ticket to be had before two years into the future. (Elvira Königsberger, alas, had not survived the transfer, her role taken by Fiona Beddoes, a granddaughter of the famous English theatrical family and already a draw in her own right. But Elvira would get credit in all the theatrical histories for having "created" the role; she starred in the original-cast recording, already a platinum CD; and she was granted a severance sum and a percentage that she would have been foolish to refuse. After her fashion, she had at last grasped the brass ring.) A movie version was already in production; the musical had by now been translated into seventeen languages; simultaneous openings had been proposed for London, Paris and Berlin; a Japanese version was nearing completion. On all El-Al international flights a saccharine rendition of the overture, all strings and a lone piano, was played before every departure and upon every arrival. Duncan, a rich man to begin with, had become a very rich man indeed. In fact, all those who had invested or participated in the original Buffa production had become rich and were to become richer.

Bruno during much of this period was unemployed, given a supernumerary role in opera only at the last minute when a reliable replacement was required. Elvira's threat seemed to have become reality. But Duncan could not hold a grudge for long. Bruno had erred badly, more fool he. A friend, however, was a friend. Duncan at length invited him to join the Broadway production, not as Dreyfus, to be sure—that role was now superbly embodied by Jesús Guevara, the Cuban-American actor, who had already made his mark in the legitimate theater and in film and who henceforward would never be able to shake himself free of his identification as Dreyfus—but in three roles per performance: Emile Zola, Dreyfus's brother Mathieu, and the officer who stripped Dreyfus of his insignia and broke his sword before his eyes. In the end, Bruno too, to his shame, made money on *Dreyfus: The Musical.*

One afternoon Bruno returned from a walk in the park to find Olga in the apartment. She was in the bedroom folding her clothes and putting them away in drawers. The lace counterpane was back on the bed.

"Hello, Bruno," she said shyly.

"Hello yourself."

"You said I should come home."

"Yes, yes I did. That was some time ago, of course. But yes."

"And now? Now *too* I should come home?"

"He wouldn't marry you?"

Olga hesitated, tears welling in her eyes. "He's already married. He's got a wife and children in Moscow, maybe more in other places."

"He told you that?"

"The FBI told me. I was arrested. They arrested us both. Oh, Bruno, I'm so ashamed, I could die."

But now the tears came. She ran sobbing into his arms. He held her, gratefully breathing in again the familiar perfume of her hair.

She mumbled something into his chest. Gently, he pushed her from him. "What?"

"He's a big crook, a gangster, a killer maybe. Yes, maybe he's killed someone. The police want him in Moscow. He'll be deported, or else he'll be prosecuted here. They broke into the apartment, the bedroom. I wanted to crawl into a hole. The FBI treated me like I was dirty, like I was a prostitute. The worst was a young blond crew-cut in his neat suit and tie and white shirt, must be a churchgoer, maybe a Mormon. You could see the disgust in his face. He said I could be deported too, I'd better watch it, consorting with known criminals."

"Didn't you know what he was?"

"He told me he was in import-export. But, yes, I got suspicious after a while, that's true. Strange people would come at any hour of the day or night. I was made to stay in the kitchen or the bedroom. Once, he sent me out of the house, told me to go to the movies."

"Why didn't you leave him?"

"Another interrogation, my hero? You should be in the FBI," said Olga sarcastically. Her eyes flashed.

The old irritability hung with delightful familiarity between them.

"Don't you want to tell me?"

"There's nothing to tell. At first he was very nice, very gentle, he treated me with respect, not like you. He said he loved me and wanted to marry me. But he would drink, Bruno, you can't imagine how much he would drink, bottle after bottle of vodka. Then he would start weeping, and then he would pass out. Sometimes, before he passed out, he would turn into an animal, a bully. He would hit me. Then the next day he would say he was sorry. I couldn't leave him, don't you see? I was afraid he'd come after me, he'd find me. He slept with a gun under his pillow." Olga searched Bruno's face for his reaction to this revelation and seemed satisfied. "No more questions. That's it. End of story."

Bruno, in fact, had heard quite enough, more than he wanted to hear. He thought to take her in his arms again and comfort her. Instead, he went very deliberately to the bed and lay on the counterpane, his shoes still on.

Olga's eyes narrowed, and she took an angry step towards him. Then she sniffed. "I'm going to take a shower," she said. But she left wearing a mysterious smile, a smile Bruno was content to interpret as triumph.

When she returned she was wrapped in a large Turkish towel that reached the floor. Thus hobbled, she ran with little steps to the bedside, dropped the towel, and stood before him, her lovely body glowing pinkly from the hot shower, the large black cross hanging between her naked breasts.

"Are you pleased to see me, my samurai?"

Bruno yawned and stretched himself luxuriously on the bed. He folded his arms behind his head on the pillow, smiled, and closed his eyes.

"The cross," he said, "will have to go."